AND
THE WORD
WAS MADE

FLETCH.

Fletch had bugged a lot of people in his time. But he'd never bugged so many at once. What with some interesting women around and some far-out orgies to eavesdrop on, Fletch was in for a wild convention. Then Walter March, publisher of a string of powerful newspapers, met a brutal demise. And at the American journalism convention, plenty of people had the motive and the opportunity.

With the best investigative reporters in the business gathered under one roof, the competition was stiff for the witty and wicked I. M. Fletcher. But Fletch had something going for him the other hacks couldn't match. Himself.

"Good, old-fashioned, page-turning fun . . . a flair that has been absent from novels of this sort since the days of vintage James Bond."

Penthouse

"Bright and entertaining . . . Fletch, as irreverent and smart as ever, is back."

The New York Times

Other Avon Books by
Gregory Mcdonald

CONFESS, FLETCH
FLETCH
FLYNN
RUNNING SCARED

Fletch's Fortune

GREGORY MCDONALD

AVON
PUBLISHERS OF BARD, CAMELOT, DISCUS AND FLARE BOOKS

FLETCH'S FORTUNE is an original publication of Avon
Books. This work has never before appeared in book form.

AVON BOOKS
A division of
The Hearst Corporation
959 Eighth Avenue
New York, New York 10019

First Avon Printing, July, 1978

FOR Susi, Chris, and Doug

One

"C.I.A., Mister Fletcher."

"Um. Would you mind spelling that?"

Coming into the cool dark of the living room, blinded by the sun on the beach, Fletch had smelled cigar smoke and slowed at the French doors.

There were two forms, of men, sprawled on his living-room furniture, one in the middle of the divan, the other on a chair.

"The Central Intelligence Agency," one of the forms muttered.

Fletch's bare feet crossed the marble floor to the carpet.

"Sorry, old chaps. You've got the wrong bod. Fletch is away for a spell. Letting me use his digs." Fletch held out his hand to the form on the divan. "Always do feel silly introducing myself whilst adorned in swimming gear, but when on the Riviera, do as the sons of habitués do—isn't that the motto? The name's Arbuthnot," Fletch said. "Freddy Arbuthnot."

The man on the divan had not shaken his hand.

The man in the chair snorted.

"Arbuthnot it's not," said the man in the chair.

"Not?" said Fletch. "Not?"

"Not," said the man.

The patterns of their neckties had become visible to Fletch.

His nose was in a stream of cigar smoke.

There were two cigar butts and a live cigar in the ash tray on the coffee table.

Next to the ash tray, on the surface of the table, was a photograph, of Fletch, in United States Marine Corps uniform, smiling.

Fletch said, "Golly."

"Didn't want to disturb you on the beach with your girl friend," said the man in the chair. "The two of you looked too cute down there. Frisking on the sand."

"Adorable," uttered the man on the divan.

Both men were dressed in full suits, collars undone, ties pulled loose.

Both their faces were wet with perspiration.

"Let's see some identification," Fletch said.

This time he held his hand out to the man in the chair, palm up.

The man looked up at Fletch a moment, into his eyes, as if to gauge the exact degree of Fletch's seriousness, then rolled left on his hams and pulled his wallet from his right rear trouser pocket.

On the left flap was the man's photograph. On the right was a card which said: "CENTRAL INTELLIGENCE AGENCY, United States of America," a few dates, a few numbers, and the man's name—Eggers, Gordon.

"You, too." Fletch held out his hand to the man on the divan.

His name was Richard Fabens.

"Eggers and Fabens." Fletch handed them back their credentials. "Would you guys mind if I got out of these wet trunks and took a shower?"

"Not at all," said Eggers, standing up. "But let's talk first."

"Coffee?"

"If we wanted coffee," said Fabens, standing up, "we would have made it ourselves."

8

"Part of the C.I.A. training, I expect," Fletch said. "Trespass and Coffee-Making. A Bloody Mary? Something to raise the spirits on this Sunday noon?"

"Cool it, Fletcher," said Eggers. "You don't need time to think." He put the tip of his index finger against Fletch's chest, and pressed. "You're going to do what you're told. Get it?"

Fletch shouted into his face, "Yes, sir!"

Suddenly Eggers' right hand became a fist and smashed into precisely the right place in Fletch's stomach with incredible force, considering the shortness of the swing.

Fletch was hunched over, in a chair, trying to breathe.

"Enough of your bull, Fletcher."

"I caught a fish like him once." Fabens was relighting his cigar. "In the Gulf Stream. He was still wriggling and fighting even after I had him aboard. I had to beat the shit out of him to convince him he was caught. Even then." He blew a billow of cigar smoke at Fletch. "Mostly I beat him on the head."

"Yuck," said Fletch.

"Shall we beat you on the head, Fletcher?" Eggers asked.

Fletch said, "Anything's better than that cigar's smoke."

Eggers' voice turned gentle. "Are you going to listen to us, Irwin?"

Fletch said, "El Cheap-o."

Turning from the French doors, El Cheap-o in mouth, Fabens asked, "What happened to your girl friend? Where'd she go?"

"Home." Fletch squeezed out breath. "She lives next door." He sucked in breath. "With her husband."

He raised his head in time to see Eggers and Fabens glance at each other.

"Husband?"

"He sleeps late," Fletch breathed. "Sundays."

"Jesus," said Eggers.

"Wriggle, wriggle," said Fabens.

Fletch straightened his back in the chair. He ignored the tears on his cheeks.

"Okay, guys. What's the big deal?"

"No big deal." Eggers rubbed his hands together. "Easy."

"You're just the right man for the job," said Fabens.

"What job?"

"You know the American Journalism Alliance?" Eggers asked.

"Yes."

"They're having a convention," Fabens said.

"So?"

"You're going."

"Hell, I'm not a working journalist anymore. I'm unemployed. I haven't worked as a journalist in over a year."

"What do you mean?" said Eggers. "You had a piece in *Bronson's* just last month."

"That was on the paintings of Cappoletti."

"So? It's journalism."

"Once a shithead, always a shithead," said Fabens.

"May your cigar kill you," said Fletch.

"You're going," said Eggers.

"I'm not even a member of the A.J.A."

"You are," said Eggers.

"I used to be."

"You are."

"I haven't paid my dues in years. In fact, I never paid my dues."

"We paid your dues. You're a member."

"You paid my dues?"

"We paid your dues."

"Very thoughtful of you," Fletch said.

"Think nothing of it," said Fabens. "Anything for a shithead."

Fletch said, "You could have spent the money on a better grade of cigars. Preferably Cuban."

"I'm a government employee." Fabens looked at the tip of his cigar. "What do you expect?"

"Peace?"

"The convention starts tomorrow," Eggers said. "Outside of Washington. In Virginia."

"Tomorrow?"

"We didn't want you to have too long to think about it."

"No way."

"Tomorrow," Fabens said. "You're going to be there."

"I'm having lunch with this guy in Genoa tomorrow. Tuesday, I'm flying down to Rome for an exhibition."

"Tomorrow," said Fabens.

"I don't have a ticket. I haven't packed."

"We have your ticket." Eggers waved his hand. "You can do your own packing."

Fletch sat forward, placing his forearms on his thighs.

"Okay," he said. "What's this about?"

"At the airport in Washington, near the Trans World Airlines' main counters, you will go to a baggage locker." Fabens took a key from his jacket pocket and looked at it. "Locker Number 719. In that locker you will find a reasonably heavy brown suitcase."

"Full of bugging equipment," said Eggers.

Fletch said, "Shit, no!"

Fabens flipped the key onto the coffee table.

"Shit, yes."

"No way!" said Fletch.

"Absolutely," said Fabens. "You will then take another airplane to Hendricks, Virginia, to the old

Hendricks Plantation, where the convention is being held, and you will immediately set out planting listening devices in the rooms of all your colleagues, if I may use such a term for you shitheads of the fourth estate."

"It's not going to happen," said Fletch.

"It's going to happen," said Fabens. "In the brown suitcase—and forgive us, we had trouble matching your luggage exactly—there is also a recording machine and plenty of tape. You are going to tape the most private, bedroom conversations of the most important people in American journalism."

"You're crazy."

Eggers shook his head. "Not crazy."

"You are crazy." Fletch stood up. "You've told me more than you should have. Bunglers! You've given me a story." Fletch grabbed the key from the coffee table. "One phone call, and this story is going to be all over the world in thirty-six hours."

Fletch backed off the carpet onto the marble floor.

"Blow smoke in my face. You're not going to get this key from me."

Fabens smiled, holding his cigar chest-height.

"We haven't told you too much. We've told you too little."

"What haven't you told me?"

Eggers shook his head, seemingly in embarrassment. "We've got something on you."

"What have you got on me? I'm not a priest or a politician. There's no way you can spoil my reputation."

"Taxes, Mister Fletcher."

"What?"

Fabens said again, "Taxes."

Fletch blinked. "What about 'em?"

"You haven't paid any."

"Nonsense. Of course I pay taxes."

"Not nonsense, Mister Fletcher." Fabens used the

ash tray. "Look at it our way. Your parents lived in the state of Washington, neither of them well-to-do nor from well-to-do families."

"They were nice people."

"I'm sure. Nice, yes. Rich, no. Yet here you are, living in a villa in Cagna, Italy, the Mediterranean sparkling through your windows, driving a Porsche ... unemployed."

"I retired young."

"In your lifetime, you have paid almost no federal taxes."

"I had expenses."

"You haven't even filed a return. Ever."

"I have a very slow accountant."

"I should think he would be slow," continued Fabens, "seeing you have money in Rio, in the Bahamas, here in Italy, probably in Switzerland. . . ."

"I also have a very big sense of insecurity," Fletch said.

"I should think you would have," Fabens said. "Under the circumstances."

"All right. I haven't paid my taxes. I'll pay my taxes, pay the penalties—but after I phone in the story that you guys are bugging the convention of the American Journalism Alliance."

"It's the not filing the tax reports that's the crime, Mister Fletcher. Punishable by jail sentences."

"So what? Let 'em catch me."

Eggers was sitting in a chair, hands behind his head, staring at Fletch.

"Peek-a-boo," Fabens said. "We have caught you."

"Bull. I can outrun you two tubs anytime."

"Mister Fletcher, do you want to know why you haven't filed any tax returns?"

"Why haven't I filed any tax returns?"

"Because you can't say where the money came from."

"I found it at the foot of my bed one morning."

Eggers laughed, turned his head to Fabens, and said, "Maybe he did."

"You should have reported it," said Fabens.

"I'll report it."

"You have never earned more than a reporter's salary—about the price of that Porsche in your driveway—in any one year . . . legally."

"Who reports gambling earnings?"

"Where did you get the money? Over two million dollars, possibly three, maybe more."

"I went scuba diving off the Bahamas and found a Spanish galleon loaded with trading stamps."

"Crime on top of crime." Fabens put his cigar stub in the ash tray. "Ten, twenty, thirty years in prison."

"Maybe by the time you get out," laughed Eggers, "the girl next door will be divorced."

"Oh, Gordon," Fabens said. "We forgot to tell Mister Irwin Maurice Fletcher that in one of my pockets I have his T.W.A. ticket to Hendricks, Virginia. In my other pocket I have his extradition papers."

Eggers slapped his kidney. "And I, Richard, have a warm pair of Italian handcuffs."

Fletch sat down.

"Gee, guys, these are my friends. You're asking me to bug my friends."

Fabens said, "I thought a good journalist didn't have any friends."

Fletch muttered, "Just other journalists."

Eggers said, "You don't have a choice, Fletcher."

"Damn." Fletch was turning the baggage locker key over in his hands. "I thought you C.I.A. guys stopped all this: domestic spying, bugging journalists. . . ."

"Who's spying?" said Eggers.

"You've got us all wrong," said Fabens. "This is simply a public relations effort. We're permitted to do public relations. All we want are a few friends in the American press."

"You never know," said Eggers. "If we know what some of their personal problems are, we might even be able to help them out."

"All we want is to be friendly," said Fabens. "Especially do we want to be friendly with Walter March. You know him?"

"Publisher. March Newspapers. I used to work for him."

"That's right. A very powerful man. I don't suppose you happen to know what goes on in his bedroom?"

"Christ," said Fletch. "He must be over seventy."

"So what," said Eggers. "I've been reading a book. . . ."

"Walter March," repeated Fabens. "We wish to make good friends with Walter March."

"So I do this thing for you, and what then?" Fletch asked. "Then I go to jail?"

"No, no. Then your tax problems disappear as if by magic. They fall in the Potomac River, never to surface again."

"How?"

"We take care of it," answered Eggers.

"Can I have that in writing?"

"No."

"Can I have anything in writing?"

"No."

Fabens put the Trans World Airlines ticket folder on the coffee table.

"Genoa, London, Washington, Hendricks, Virginia. Your plane leaves at four o'clock."

Fletch looked at his sunburned arm.

"I need a shower."

Eggers laughed. "Putting on a pair of pants wouldn't hurt any, either."

Fabens said, "I take it you choose to go home without handcuffs?"

Fletch said, "Does Pruella the pig pucker her pussy when she poops in the woods?"

Two

"So you're going to bug the entire American press establishment? Just because someone asked you to?"

Gibbs' voice was barely audible. Fletch had had a better connection when he had called from London.

Across the National Airport waiting room a brass quartet was beginning to play "America."

Fletch pushed the brown suitcase he had taken from Locker Number 719 out of the telephone booth with his foot and slammed the door.

"Fletch?"

"Hello? I was closing the door."

"Are you in Washington now?"

"Yes."

"Did you have a nice flight?"

"No."

"Sorry to hear that. Why not ?"

"Sat next to a Methodist minister."

"What's wrong with sitting next to a Methodist minister?"

"Are you kidding? The closer to heaven we got, the smugger he got."

"Jesus, Fletch."

"That's what I say."

"Can you still sing a few bars of the old North-western fight song?"

"Never could."

In college, Don Gibbs had believed in the football team (he was a second-string tackle), beer (a case between Saturday night and Monday morning), the Chevrolet car (he had a sedan, painted blue and yellow), the Methodist Church (for women and children), and applied physics (for an eventual guaranteed income from American industry, which he also believed in, but which, upon his graduation, had not returned his faith by offering him a job). He had not believed in poetry, painting, philosophy, people, or any of the other *p*'s treated in the humanities—an attitude generally accepted by American industry, but not when manifested by the candidate for a job so obviously.

He and Fletch had been roommates in their freshman year.

"The only thing I learned in college," Fletch said into the phone, "is that all our less successful classmates went to work for the government."

"Who placed this call?" Gibbs' throat muscles had tightened. "Tell me that, Fletcher. Did you call me, or did I call you? Are you asking me to help you, or am I asking you to help me?"

"Gee whiz, Don. You forgot to take your Insensitive Pill this morning."

"I'm sick to death of you guys knocking us in the press whenever you feel like it, but whenever you have a problem that hurts even a little bit you're crying over the phone at us."

"Bullshit, Don. I've never knocked you in the press. You've never been important enough to knock."

"Oh, yeah?"

They might as well have been seventeen-year-old freshmen arguing at eleven o'clock at night over who got to take a shower first. Fletch always hated to wait twenty minutes while Gibbs went through his shower routine; Gibbs hated the mirrors steamed by the time he got to take his shower.

Fletch said, "Yeah. Furthermore, I'm not asking you a favor. I'm asking you a question."

"What's the question, Irwin Maurice? Do you have the legal right to bug the entire American press establishment? No! Absolutely not." His voice lowered. "But then again, Irwin Maurice Fletcher, I suspect you always have bugged the entire American press establishment."

"Funny, funny." He had to grant that; he had to give him something. "Since when are you a lawyer? I'm not asking for legal advice. I know it's not nice to bug my friends with the intention of blackmail—even if I'm not the guy who's going to be putting the screws to 'em— you shits are. My question is: Do I have to do this?"

There was a long silence from the other end of the phone.

Fletch said, "Hello? Don?"

The line clicked.

"Fletch?"

"Hello."

"I'm trying to answer your question. Would you mind going over all the facts again?"

Don Gibbs' voice had moderated. It had become more mature, reasonable, responsible. It also had lowered half an octave.

"I gave you all the facts when I called you from London, Don."

"Just to make sure I've got everything straight."

"You're just trying to take advantage of a local phone call from an old friend to make you look busy at your desk," Fletch said. "Bastard."

Fletch knew it wasn't a local phone call.

The number he had dialed supposedly was a Pentagon number. But he knew he was talking to Don Gibbs in that curious underground headquarters of American intelligence in the mountains of North Carolina.

"I have a plane to catch."

"Just run it by me again, Fletch."

"Okay. Two of your goons broke into my house in Cagna, Italy, yesterday morning, Sunday—"

"Names?"

"Gordon Eggers and Richard Fabens."

"Eggers, Gordon and Fabens, Richard. Right?"

"You government jerks do everything backwards."

"Did you get their identification numbers off their credentials?"

"No. But they had numbers. Lots of numbers."

"Doesn't matter. When you say they broke into your house, what precisely do you mean?"

"I think they entered through the French windows, doors, whatever you call them. The house was open."

"Did they actually break anything?"

"Amazingly enough—no."

"So they entered your house."

"They entered it uninvited. Unexpected. Unwanted. They trespassed."

"What are you doing with a house in Italy?"

"I live there."

"Yeah, but why? I mean, are you working for a wire service or something?"

"No. I'm doing some writing on art. I had a piece in *Bronson's* last month. I'm trying to do a biography of Edgar Arthur Tharp, Junior. . . ."

"The cowboys-and-Indian artist?"

"Gee. You know something."

"Wasn't he a friend of Winslow Homer?"

"No."

"Have you given up investigative reporting altogether?"

Fletch dropped a pause into the conversation. "I'm on a sabbatical."

"Fired again, uh? I'm glad I'm not one of the more obvious successes in my class."

"There's no job security," Fletch said, "without complete obscurity."

"So what did these two gentlemen want?"

"They weren't gentlemen."

"Sorry to hear that. We usually send only our finest abroad. I haven't made it yet."

"Not surprised."

"What did they want?"

Across the terminal the band was playing "The eyes of Texas are upon you. . . ."

"They told me to come to the A.J.A. convention, here in Hendricks, Virginia, and bug my ever-loving colleagues—get tape recordings of their bedroom conversations—and turn the tapes over to them, for blackmail purposes. They said there would be a suitcase full of bugging equipment here in a locker in Washington, and it is here." Through the door of the phone booth Fletch noticed how badly the suitcase he had just taken from Locker 719 matched the rest of his luggage. "Are you telling me you don't know all this already, Don?"

Don Gibbs said, "It's not often we get another perspective on one of our operations."

"When I called you from London last night, I asked you to look into all this."

"I have," Don said. "I've checked pretty thoroughly."

"So why am I standing in a phone booth, late for a plane I don't want to take anyway, going over it all with you again?"

"Tell me again why you agreed to do it. I just want to see if it checks out with what I know."

"Oh, for God's sake, Don! I'm being blackmailed."

"I know that, but tell me again how."

21

"Well. . . ."

"It won't hurt to tell me, Fletcher. Don't I already know?"

"Nice guy." The floor of the phone booth was filthy. "Taxes."

"You've never paid any?"

"Just whatever was withheld from my salary." He was pressing the phone against his ear. "Even for those years I never filed a return."

"Uh-uh. And what about the last year or two?"

"I've never filed a return."

"It says here you have money you can't account for. Is that right?"

"Yeah."

"What?"

"Yes."

"So why are you calling me?"

"You're my friend in the American Intelligence community."

"We're not friends."

"Acquaintance. I'm trying to report to someone in the home office—someone responsible—that your guys down the line are blackmailing me to bug the private lives of some of the most important members of the American press—newspapers, radio, and television."

"Don't you think our right hand knows what our left hand is doing?"

"No, I don't. And if you do, you should be ashamed of yourselves."

"I'm not ashamed of myself. Nobody's blackmailing me."

"Come on, Don! Jesus Christ!"

"How do you think we gather intelligence, Fletcher? By reading your lousy newspapers? From network news?"

"Don, this isn't legitimate, and you know it."

"I know lots of things." Gibbs' voice had risen again, slightly. "You said when you called from London that the guys who talked to you were particularly interested in getting information on old Mister March."

"Yes. That's right. Walter March. I used to work for him."

"What does that mean to you?"

"That they single out March?"

"Yes."

"He's an incredibly powerful man. March Newspapers." Fletch's right ear was becoming hot and sore. "Listen, Don, I've only got a few minutes to make that plane, if I'm going to make it. Are you telling me . . . ?"

"No, Mister Fletcher. I'm telling you."

It was a much older, deeper voice.

"Who is this?" Fletch asked.

"Robert Englehardt," the voice said. "Don's department head. I've been listening in."

"Man!" Alone in the phone booth, Fletch grinned. "You guys can't do anything straight."

"I guess you're calling Don to ask if this assignment is something you have to take on."

"You've got it."

"What do you think the answer is?"

"It sounds to me like the answer is yes."

"You have the right impression."

There was another click on the line.

Fletch asked, "Don, are you still there?"

"Yes."

"I know you guys are so wrapped up in your own mysteriousness you can't answer a simple question yes or no, but why the extra degree of mysteriousness about this?"

"What mysteriousness?"

"Come on, Don."

"We've just been trying to make absolutely sure that the A.J.A. convention is still on."

"Still on? Why wouldn't it be?"

"You journalists are always the last with the news, aren't you?"

"What news?"

"Walter March was murdered this morning. At the convention. So long, Fletcher."

Three

"Hello, hello," Fletch said, as he buckled himself into the seat next to the girl with the honey-colored hair and the brown eyes. "I get along well with everybody."

"You don't even get along with plane schedules," she answered. "They've been holding the plane for you for ten minutes."

It was a twelve-seater.

"I was on the phone," Fletch said. "Talking to an old uncle. He doesn't talk as fast as he used to."

The pilot slammed the passenger door and pulled the handle up.

"I forgive you," the girl said. "Why are you so tan?"

"I just arrived from Italy. This morning."

"That would have been excuse enough."

The pilot had started the engines and turned the plane away from the terminal.

"Ask me if I had a nice flight."

They had to shout. The plane had three propellers, one of them right over their heads.

"Did you have a nice flight?"

"No." Taxiing to the runway, the small plane was very bouncy. "Ask me why I didn't have a nice flight."

"Why didn't you have a nice flight?"

"I sat next to a Methodist minister."

She said, "So what?"

"The closer to heaven we got, the smugger he got."

She shook her head. "Jet lag affects different people in different ways."

Fletch said, "My uncle didn't think it was funny either."

"Not only that," the girl said, "but telling it to your uncle probably took up the whole ten minutes we waited."

"I'm a loyal nephew."

The plane stopped. Each of the three engines was gunned. With the left engine still running high, the brakes were released and the plane swung onto the runway. Gathering speed, it bounced and vibrated down the runway until the bounces got big enough, at which point the plane popped into the air.

The plane rose and banked over Washington and the sound of the engines diminished somewhat.

The girl was looking out her window.

She said, "I love to look at Washington from the air. Such a pretty place."

"Want to buy it?"

She gave him the sardonic grin he deserved. "You say you get along well with everybody?"

"Everybody," Fletch said. "Absolutely everybody. Methodist ministers, uncles, terrific looking girls sitting next to me on airplanes . . ."

"Am I terrific looking?" she shouted.

"Smashing."

"You mean smash-mirrors kind of smashing?"

"I dunno. Maybe. How's your husband?"

"Don't have one."

"Why not?"

"Never found anybody good enough to marry me. How's your wife?"

"Which one?"

"You have lots?"

"Have had. Lots and lots. Gross lots. Practically anybody's good enough to marry me."

"Guess that lets me out," she said.

"I ask people to marry me too quickly," Fletch said. "At least that's what the Methodist minister said."

"And they all say yes?"

"Most have. It's a thing with me. I love the old institutions. Like marriage."

"It's a problem?"

"Definitely. Will you help me with it?"

"Of course."

"When I ask you to marry me, please say no."

"Okay."

Fletch looked at his wristwatch and counted off ten seconds under his breath.

"Will you marry me?" he asked.

"Sure."

"What?"

"I said, 'Sure.' "

"Well, you're not much of a help."

"Why should I help you? You get along well with everybody."

"Don't you?"

"No."

"I can see why not. Underneath that terrific exterior, you're weird."

"It's a defense mechanism. I've been working on it."

"Have you ever been in Hendricks, Virginia, before?" Fletch asked.

"No."

"Are you going to the A.J.A. Convention?"

"Yes."

Fletch thought most, if not all, the people on the plane were.

Two seats in front of him was Hy Litwack, anchorman for United Broadcasting Company.

Even the back of Hy Litwack's head was recognizable as Hy Litwack.

"Are you a journalist?" Fletch asked.

"You think I'm a busboy?"

"No." Fletch considered his thumbs in his lap. "I hadn't thought that. You're a newsperson."

"With *Newsworld* magazine."

"Women's stuff? Fashion? Food?"

"Crime," she said, looking straight ahead.

"Women's stuff."

Fletch was smiling behind his hand.

"Newspersons' stuff. I've just come back from covering the Pecuchet trial, in Arizona."

Fletch did not know of the case.

"What was the verdict?" he asked.

She said, "Good story."

"Yee." He slapped himself on the cheek. "Yee."

She looked into his eyes. "I wouldn't expect any other verdict."

"Do you know Walter March was murdered this morning?"

"I heard about it from the taxi radio on the way to the airport. Do you have any of the details?"

"Nary a one."

"Well." She straightened her legs as much as they could be straightened in the cramped airplane. "I have two notebooks. And three pens." Touching her fingers to her lips, she yawned. "And are you a journalist?" she asked. "Or a busboy?"

"I'm not sure," he answered. "I'm on a sabbatical."

"From what company?"

"Practically all of them."

"You're unemployed," she said. "Therefore you're working on a book."

28

"You've got it."

"On the Vatican?"

"Why the Vatican?"

"You're working on the book in Italy."

"I'm working on a book about Edgar Arthur Tharp, Junior."

"You're working on a book about an American cowboy painter in Italy?"

"It brings a certain perspective to the work. Detachment."

"And, I suspect, about thirty tons of obstacles."

"Do obstacles come by the ton?"

"In your case, I think so. The rest of us measure them in kilograms."

She put her hand on his on the armrest, slipped one of her fingers under two of his, raised them and let them fall.

"I think I detect," she said, "what with all your ex-wives and ex-employers, that your life lacks a certain consistency—a certain glue."

"Rescue me," Fletch said. "Save me from myself."

"What's your name?"

"I. M. Fletcher."

"Fletcher? Never heard of you. Why so pompous about it?"

"Pompous?"

"You announced your name, *I am Fletcher*. As if someone had said you weren't. Why didn't you just say, *Fletcher?*"

She was still playing with his fingers.

"My first initial is *I*. My second initial is *M*."

"Hummmm," she said. "An affliction since birth. Does the *I* stand for Irving?"

"Worse. Irwin."

"I like the name Irwin."

"No one likes the name Irwin."

"You're just prejudiced," she said.

"I have every reason to be."

"You have nice hands."

"One on the end of each arm."

With her two hands she made a loose fist out of his left hand, brought it a few inches closer to her, and dropped it.

She was still looking at his hand.

"Would you run your hands over my naked body, time and again?"

"Here? Now?"

"Later," she said. "Later."

"I thought you'd never ask. Shall I send them in to you by Room Service, or come myself?"

"Just your hands," she said. "I don't know much about the rest of you—except that you get along well with everybody."

He took her hand in his, and she put her left hand on top of his.

She had pulled her legs into her seat.

"Ms., you have me at a disadvantage."

"I sincerely hope so."

"I don't know your name."

"Arbuthnot," she said.

"Arbuthnot!" He extricated his hand. "Not Arbuthnot!"

"Arbuthnot," she said.

"Arbuthnot?"

"Arbuthnot. Fredericka Arbuthnot."

"Freddie Arbuthnot?"

"You've heard of me? Behind that Italian tan, I detect a sudden whiteness of pallor."

"Heard of you? I made you up!"

The plane was on its landing run into Hendricks Airport.

She truly looked puzzled.
"I don't get it," she said.
"Well, I do."
Fletch unclasped his seat belt.
He said again, "I do."

Four

Mrs. Jake Williams—Helena, she insisted people call her—the hostess at the American Journalism Alliance Convention—had a way of greeting people as if they were delighted to see her.

"Fletcher, darling! Aren't you beautiful!"

She extended both hands beyond her bosom.

"Hi, Helena, how are you doing?"

He leaned over her and kissed her.

They were standing near the reception desk in the hotel lobby.

An airport limousine had been waiting for them when their airplane had touched down.

Ignoring his luggage, Fletch had gone directly to the limousine and sat in it.

In a few moments, a quiet Fredericka Arbuthnot opened the car door and slid in next to him.

After the luggage had been stowed on top of the car and most of the other passengers from the airplane had taken seats, they left the airport, went through a small village blighted by a shopping center and straight out a rolling road to the plantation.

Almost immediately outside the village were the plantation's white rail fences, on both sides of the road.

Fletch lowered his head to look through the windshield as the car turned into the plantation driveway.

On both sides of the driveway was a golf course. A

brightly dressed foursome was on a green down to the left. The car came to a full stop to let a pale blue golf cart cross the gravel driveway.

The plantation house was a mammoth red-brick structure behind a white, wooden colonnade, with matching red-brick additions at both sides and, Fletch supposed, to the rear. They were motel-type units, but well-designed, perfectly in keeping with the main house, the rolling green, the distant white fences.

On the last curve before the house, Fletch glimpsed through the side window a corner of a sparkling blue swimming pool.

No one had said a word during the ride.

The driver's polite question, aimed at the passengers in general, "Did you all have a nice flight?" when he first got into the car received no answer whatsoever.

It was if they were going to a funeral, rather than a convention.

Well, they were going to a funeral.

Walter March was dead.

He had been murdered that morning at Hendricks Plantation.

Walter March had been in his seventies. Forever, it seemed, he had been publisher of a large string of powerful newspapers.

Probably everyone in the car, at one point or another in their careers, had had dealings with Walter March.

Probably almost everyone at the convention had.

These were journalists—some of the best in the business.

Smiling to himself, Fletch realized that if any one of them—including himself—had been alone in the car with the driver, the driver would have been pumped for every bit of information, speculation, and rumor regarding the murder at his imagination's command.

Together, they asked no questions.

33

Unless in an open press conference, where there was no choice, no journalist wants to ask a question whose answer might benefit any other journalist.

Fletch waited until his luggage was handed to him from the top of the car, and then went directly into the lobby.

While Helena Williams was greeting Fletch, Fredericka Arbuthnot, with her luggage, came and stood beside him.

She was continuing to look at him quizzically.

"Hello, Mrs. Fletcher," Helena said, shaking Freddie's hand.

"This isn't Mrs. Fletcher," Fletch said.

"Oh, I'm sorry," Helena said. "We're all so used to greeting anyone with Fletch as Mrs. Fletcher."

"This is Freddie Arbuthnot."

"Freddie? So many of your girls have had boys' names," Helena said. "That girl we met with you in Italy, Andy something or other. . . ."

"Barbara and Linda," Fletch said. "Joan. . . ."

"There must be something odd about you I've never detected," she said.

"There is," said Freddie Arbuthnot.

"Furthermore, Helena," Fletch said. "Ms. Arbuthnot and I just met on the plane."

"That's never been a major consideration before," Helena sniffed. "I remember that time we were all having dinner together in New York, and I noticed you were looking at a girl at the next table, and she was looking at you, and next thing we knew, you were both gone! You hadn't even excused yourself. Not a word! I remember you missed the *tarte aux cerises, flambée.*"

"I did not."

"Well, anyway," Helena said to Freddie, "just like everything else Fletch does, he is the most spectacular dues-payer. He's coughed up every dime he's owed the American Journalism Alliance lo these many years. . . ."

"She knows," Fletch said.

"We were all staggered, Fletch darling."

"I was a little surprised myself," Fletch said. "Don't let word get around, okay, Helena? Might ruin my reputation."

"Fletch darling," Helena said, with mock sincerity, hand on his forearm, "nothing could do that."

Fletch said, "I'm sorry about Walter March, Helena."

Helena Williams pushed the mental button for A Distraught Expression.

"The crime of the century," she said. She had been married to Jake Williams, managing editor of a New York daily, for more years than anyone who knew Jake could believe. "The crime of the century, Fletch."

"Hell of a story," Freddie muttered.

"We had a vote this morning, those of us who were here, to decide if we would continue the convention. We decided to open it on time. Well, with all these people coming, what could we do? Everything's arranged. Anyway, the police asked everybody who was here to stay. Having the convention running will help take everybody's mind off this terrible tragedy. Walter March!" She threw her hands in the air. "Who'd believe it?"

"Is Lydia here, Helena?" Fletch asked.

"She found the body! She was in the bath, and she heard gurgling! She thought Walter had left the suite. At first, she said, she thought it was the tub drain. But the gurgling kept up, from the bedroom. She got out of the tub and threw a towel around herself. There was Walter, half-kneeling, fallen on one of the beds, arms thrown out, a scissors sticking up from his back! While she watched, he rolled sideways off the bed, and landed on his back! The scissors must have been driven fur-

35

ther in. She said he arched up, and then relaxed. All life had gone out of him."

Helena's expression of shock and grief was no longer the result of mental button-pushing. She was a lady genuinely struggling to comprehend what had happened, and why, and to control herself until she could.

"Poor Lydia!" she said. "She had no idea what to do. She came running down the corridor in her towel and banged on my door. I was just up. This was just before eight o'clock this morning, mind you. There was Lydia at my door, in a towel, at the age of seventy, her mouth open, and her eyes closing! I sat her down on my unmade bed, and she fell over! She fainted! I went running to their suite to get Walter. I was in my dressing gown. There was Walter on the floor, spread-eagled, eyes staring straight up. Naturally, I'd thought he'd had a heart attack or something. I didn't see any blood. Well, I thought I was going to faint. I heard someone shrieking. They tell me it was I who was shrieking." Helena looked away. Her fingers touched her throat. "I'm not so sure."

Fletch said, "Is there anything I can get you, Helena? Anything I can do for you?"

"No," she said. "I had brandy before breakfast. Quite a sizable dose. And then no breakfast. And then the house doctor here, what's-his-name, gave me one of those funny pills. My head feels like there's a yellow balloon in it. I've had tea and toast."

She smiled at them.

"Enough of this," she said. "It won't bring Walter back. Now you must tell me all about yourself, Fletch. Whom are you working for now?"

"The C.I.A."

He looked openly at Freddie Arbuthnot.

"I'm here to bug everybody."

"You've always had such a delightful sense of humor," Helena said.

"He's bugging me," Freddie muttered.

"I've heard that joke," Fletch snapped.

"Would you children like to share a room?" Helena asked. "We are sort of crowded—"

"Definitely not," Fletch said. "I suspect she snores."

"I do not."

"How do you know?"

"I've been told."

"Well, you're just so beautiful together," Helena said. "What is one supposed to think? Oh, there's Hy Litwack. I didn't see him come in. I must go say hello. Remind him he's giving the after-dinner speech tonight."

Helena episcopally put her hands on Fletch's and Freddie's hands, as if she were confirming them, or ordaining them, or marrying them.

"We must have life," she said, "in the presence of death."

Helena Williams walked away to greet Hy Litwack.

"And death," Fletch said, softly, "in the presence of life."

Five

In his room, Fletch, still wet from his shower, sat on the edge of his bed and opened the suitcase he had taken from Locker 719 at Washington's National Airport.

Through the wall he heard Fredericka Arbuthnot's hair drier in the next room.

A porter had led them through a door at the side of the lobby, down a few stairs, around a corner, and along the corridor of one of the plantation house's wings. Fletch carried his own bags.

The porter stopped at Room 77, put down Freddie's luggage, and put the key in the lock.

"Where's my room?" Fletch asked.

"Right next door, sir. Room 79."

"Oh, no."

Over the porter's shoulder, Freddie grinned at him.

"Give me my key," Fletch said.

The porter handed it to him.

"You know," Fletch said to Freddie, "for someone who's a figment of my imagination, you cling real good."

She said, "Your luggage doesn't match."

There were four doors to his room—one from the corridor, locked doors to the rooms each side of his, and one leading outdoors.

Before he took his shower, he had opened the sliding

glass doors. Before him was the swimming pool, sparsely populated by women and children. To the left was a bank of six tennis courts, only two of which were being used.

Every square centimeter of the suitcase's interior was being used.

In the center was the tape recorder, with the usual buttons, cigarette-pack-size speakers each side. It was already loaded with fresh tape. In the pocket of the suitcase lid were thirty-five more reels of tape—altogether enough for a total of seventy-two hours of taping.

Across the top of the suitcase, over the tape recorder, were two bands of stations, each having its own numbered button, each row having twelve stations. To the right was a fine tuner; to the left an ON-OFF-VOLUME dial.

In a pocket to the left of the tape recorder was a clear plastic bag of nasty-looking little bugs. Fletch shook them onto his bedspread. There were twenty-four of them, each numbered on its base.

Fletch tested one against his bedside lamp and proved to himself the bug's base was magnetic.

Below the tape recorder was a deep slot, about a centimeter wide, running almost the length of the suitcase. Toward each end were finger holes. Fletch inserted his index fingers, crooked them as much as space allowed, and pulled up—perfectly ordinary rabbit ears, telescopic antennae.

And in a pocket to the right of the tape recorder were a wire and a plug and an extension cord.

Nowhere—not on the tape recorder, nor the tape reels, not even on the suitcase—was a manufacturer's name.

Fletch extended the antennae, plugged the machine

into a wall socket, turned it on, chose bug Number 8, put it against the bedside lamp, pressed the button for station Number 8, pushed the RECORD button, and said the following:

"Attention Eggers, Gordon and Fabens, Richard!" The red volume-level needle was jumping at the sound of his voice. The machine was working. Fletch turned the volume dial a little counterclockwise. "This is your friend, Irwin Maurice Fletcher, talking to you from the beautiful Hendricks Plantation, in Hendricks, Virginia, U.S. of A. It's not my practice, of course, to accept press junkets; but, seeing your insistence I take this particular trip was totally irresistible, I want to tell you how grateful I am to you for not sending me anyplace slummy."

Fletch released the RECORD button, pushed the RE-WIND and PLAY buttons.

His own voice was so loud it made him jump to turn the VOLUME dial for counterclockwise. A very sensitive instrument.

He listened through what he had said so far.

Chuckling to himself, Fletch turned the machine off and padded in his towel to the bathroom for a glass of water before sitting on the edge of his bed and pushing the RECORD button again.

"Obviously," he said to the room at large, "I could fill up seventy-two hours of tape with jokes, stories, songs, and tap dancing but, if I understand correctly, that is not why I am here.

"In the event of my death, or whatever, I want anyone who discovers this formidable machine in my room to understand what it is doing here, and what I am doing here.

"I am being blackmailed by the Central Intelligence Agency—under threat of spending twenty years or more in prison, for failing to file federal income tax returns, illegally exporting money from the United States, plus, not being able to account for the source of the money in the first place—to bug and record the private conversations of my colleagues at the American Journalism Alliance Convention at Hendricks Plantation.

"Who'd ever think having a fortune could be so much trouble?

"My three reasons for going along with this quote assignment unquote are obvious to any journalist.

"To Eggers, Gordon, Fabens, Richard, Gibbs, Don, Englehardt, Robert, and all you other backwards people whose asses are where your mouths are supposed to be, so far I have the following to tell you.

"First, I suspect you all suck goats' cocks and lay hens.

"Second, the person you are most interested in having me bug, old Walter March, is dead. So there.

"Which, of course, causes me to wonder if the reason for your interest in him and the reason for his murder have anything in common.

"Third, Fredericka Arbuthnot has done a terrific job of clinging to me so far. She is magnificently seductive. However, you guys have to be some kind of special stupid. What you've done is like sending a man into battle with an arrow through his head.

"More jokes and stories later. I'll try to learn all the verses of 'The Wreck of the *Edmund Fitzgerald*' to sing to you at bedtime."

Fletch turned the machine off and sat another moment, hands in lap, looking at it.

Then he put the suitcase on the floor, leaving it open, and slid it under the bed with his toe. Kneeling, he forced the antennae under the box spring.

He lay on his stomach on the floor, unplugged the

41

machine, and shoved all the wire under the bed, so none of it would be visible from anywhere in the room, and replugged it, running the wire between the bed's headboard and the wall.

Wriggling out from under the bed, his left biceps landed on paper—an envelope.

Sitting cross-legged on the floor, he picked up the envelope. He was sure it had not been there before. It must have fallen out of the suitcase. It had not been sealed.

Dear Mister Fletcher:

Our representatives in Italy, in explaining your assignment to you, mentioned only the name of Mister Walter March.

As you have now seen, the equipment we provided you has twenty-four listening devices and stations. We would like to have our public relations effort directed specifically at those on the following list. You may disperse the remainder of the listening devices in the quarters of those younger journalists you feel are most apt to rise to positions of power and influence, in time. We will not consider this assignment completed unless all the devices have been used profitably. . . .

Next to each name on the list was the journalist's network, wire service, newspaper, or magazine affiliation.

They were all so well known there was absolutely no need to list their affiliations.

On the list were Mr. and Mrs. Walter March, Walter March, Junior, Leona Hatch, Robert McConnell, Rolly Wisham, Lewis Graham, Hy Litwack, Sheldon Levi, Mr. and Mrs. Jake Williams, Nettie Horn, Frank Gillis,

Tom Lockhart, Richard Baldridge, Stuart Poynton, Eleanor Earles, and Oscar Perlman.

"Sonsabitches," Fletch said. "Sonsabitches."

There was no signature, of course—just the words, in tiny print at the very bottom of the letter, "WE USE RECYCLED PAPER."

Six

Fletch picked up the ringing telephone and said, "Thank you for calling."

"Is this Ronald Albemarle Blodgett Islington Dimwitty Fletcher?" a woman's voice asked.

"Why, no," Fletch answered. "It isn't."

Who would be calling him *rabid*?

He remembered vaguely an old joke someone had once told about Fletch biting a dog on a slow news night.

Who else?

"Crystal!" he said. "My pal, my ass! How the hell are you?"

Giggling. Per usual. In her throat. Per usual. Sardonically silly old Crystal.

"Are you here?" he asked. "Has the Crystal Palace shivered and shimmied into my very own purview?"

She began to sing the words, "All of me...." He joined in halfway through the first bar.

"Still heavily concerned with your tonnage, eh, old girl? Still down in the chins?"

Crystal Faoni was not pellucid. She, too, had been cursed by her parents when it had come time to delete "Baby Girl Faoni" from the birth register and substitute something more specific.

Crystal was dark, with black hair which could have been straight, or could have been curly, but wasn't either; blessedly, basically heavy, with monumental bones, each demanding its kilogram of flesh; the appetite of a bear just after the first snowfall.

She also had huge, wide-set brown eyes, the world's most gorgeous skin, and a mind so sprightly and entertaining apparently it had never felt the need to cause her body to do anything but the sedentary.

She and Fletch had worked together on a newspaper in Chicago.

"Are you well?" he asked.

"I thought we could meet in the bar before the Welcoming Cocktail Party, and have too much to drink."

"I plan to go sit in the sauna and have a rub." Skimming the hotel's brochure on the bedside table, Fletch had noticed there were an exercise room, a sauna, and a massage room open from ten to seven.

"Oh, Fletch," she said. "Why do you always have to be doing such healthy things?"

"I've been on airplanes and in airports the last twenty-four hours. I'm stiff."

"You've already had too much to drink? You don't sound it."

"Not that way. Are you still working in Chicago?"

"Why," she asked rhetorically, "do people go to conventions?"

"To wear funny hats and blow raspberry noisemakers?"

"No."

"I don't know, Crystal. I've never been to a convention before."

"Why are you here, I. M. Fletcher?"

Lord love a duck, he said to himself. Everyone who knew him would know that convention-going was not his thing.

Neither was dues-paying.

He said, "Ah. . . ."

"Let me guess. You're unemployed, right?"

"Between jobs."

"Right. Let's return to our original question: Why do people go to conventions?"

"To get jobs?"

"About half. Either to get jobs, if they are unemployed, or to get better jobs, if they are employed."

"Yes."

"About a third of the people at conventions are looking for people to hire. A convention, dear Mister Fletcher, as you well know, is one great meat market. And, as I don't need to remind you, I am one great piece of meat."

"If memory serves, you do help fill up a room."

"It is not possible to overlook me."

"What about the other sixteen-point-seven percent?"

"What?"

"You said half the people are here to get jobs and a third are here to give jobs. That leaves sixteen-point-seven percent. Almost. What are they doing here?"

"Oh. Those are the people who will drop anything they are doing, including nothing, at any time, and go anywhere, for any reason, at someone else's expense, preferably, their company's."

"Gotcha."

"Except for poor little Crystal Faoni, who is here—as I expect you are—by the grace of a rapidly dwindling savings account."

"Crystal, how did you know I'm unemployed?"

"Because if you were employed you would be working on a story somewhere, and no one could divert you to attend a convention even under threat of execution. About right?"

"Now, Crystal, you know I always do what I'm told."

"Remember that time they found you asleep under the serving counter in the paper's cafeteria?"

46

"I had worked late."

"But, Fletch, you weren't alone. One of the all-night telephone operators was with you."

"So what?"

"At least you had your jeans on, all zipped up nicely. That was all you were wearing."

"We had fallen asleep."

"I guess. Jack Saunders was absolutely purple. The cafeteria staff refused to work that day. . . ."

"People get upset over the most trivial things."

"My missing lunch, Fletcher, is not a trivial thing. If you had been working for old man March at that point, you would have been fired before you reached for your shirt."

"You worked on a March newspaper, didn't you?"

"In Denver. And I was fired from it. On moral grounds."

"Moral grounds? You?"

"Me."

"What did you do, overdose on banana splits?"

"You know all about it."

"I do not."

"Everyone knows all about it."

"I don't."

"No, I suppose you don't. I don't suppose anyone would bother to pass on such a juicy piece of moral scandal to you. You're the source of so many such scandals yourself. You'd just say 'Ho hum' and gun your motorcycle."

"Ho hum," Fletch said.

"You know, instead of being on the telephone all this time, we could be curled in a dark corner of the bar, tossing down mint juleps or whatever the poison of the house is."

"Are you going to tell me?"

"I was pregnant."

47

"How could anyone tell?"

"Pardon me while I chuckle."

"Were you married?"

"Of course not."

"So why was that Walter March's business?"

"I didn't act contrite enough. I had told people I intended to have the baby, and keep it. That was back it those days. Remember? We all thought things had changed?"

"Yeah."

"I had gotten pregnant on purpose, of course. An absolutely great guy. Phil Shapiro. Remember him?"

"No."

"An absolutely great guy. Good-looking. Brainy. Happily married."

"So what happened to the kid? The baby?"

"I thought I could handle having a baby without being married. But I sure couldn't handle having a baby without being either married or employed."

"Abortion?"

"Yeah."

"Shit."

"That's what happened to my savings account the last time it got over two thousand dollars."

"Great old Walter March."

"He fired a great many people on moral grounds."

"Oddly enough, he never fired me."

"He never caught you. Or probably he heard so much about you, he never believed any of it. Even I can't believe everything I've heard about you."

"None of it is true."

"I was there that morning they found you under the cafeteria counter. And I hadn't had breakfast."

"Sorry."

"So whoever stuck the scissors into noble old Walter March was inspired."

"Did you?"

"I'd be pleased to be accused."

"You probably will be. You fit into the category of people who had a motive. He took a child away from you. Were you here this morning?"

"Yes."

"You had the opportunity to kill him?"

"I suppose so. Lydia said the door to the suite was open when she found him. Anyone could have walked in and scissored him."

"What else do you know about the murder, Crystal?"

"That it's going to be the best reported crime in history. There are more star reporters at Hendricks Plantation at this moment than have ever been gathered under one roof before. In fact, I suspect more are showing up unexpectedly, simply because of the murder. Do you realize what it would be worth to a person's career to scoop the murder of Walter March—with all this competition around?"

"Yeah."

"It would be worth more than a handful of Pulitzer Prizes."

"Whose scissors was it? Do you know?"

"Someone took it from the hotel desk. The reception desk."

"Oh."

"You thought you had the murder solved already, eh, Fletcher?"

"Well, I was thinking. Not many people carry scissors with them when they travel—at least ones big enough to stab someone—and anyone who would carry scissors that big most likely would be a woman. . . ."

"Fletcher, you must get rid of this chauvinism of yours. I've talked to you before about this."

"It's a moot point now anyway, if the scissors came from the hotel desk, where anybody could palm them."

"Anyway," Crystal said. "It's hilarious. All the reporters are running around, pumping everybody. The switchboard is all jammed up with outgoing calls. I doubt there's a keyhole in the whole hotel without an ear to it."

"Yeah," Fletch said. "Funny."

"You go have your rub, sybarite. Will I see you at the Welcoming Cocktail Party?"

"You bet," Fletch said. "I wouldn't miss it for all the juleps in Virginia."

"You'll be able to recognize me," Crystal said. "I'll be wearing my fat."

Seven

"Another one," the masseuse said.

Fletch was lying on his back on the massage table.

She was working on the muscles in his right leg.

He had been told he would have to wait more than an hour for the masseur to be free.

The masseuse was a big blond in her fifties. She looked Scandinavian, but her name was Mrs. Leary.

He had waited until she was finished with his right arm before mentioning Walter March.

His question was: "Did Walter March come in for a massage last night?"

The masseuse said, "I'm beginning to understand just how you reporters operate. How you get what you write. What do you call 'em? Sources. Sources for what you write. You're always quoting some big expert or other. 'Sources.' Huh! Now I see you all just rush to some little old lady rubbin' bones in the basement and ask her about everything. I'm no expert, Mister, on anything. And I'm no source."

Fletch looked down the length of himself at the muscles in her arms.

"Experts," he said, "are the sources of opinions. People are the sources of facts."

"Uh." She dug her fingers into his thigh. "Well, I'm no source of either facts or opinions. I'll tell you one thing. I've never been so busy. You're the ninth re-

51

porter I've massaged today, every one of 'em wanting me to talk about Mister March. I suppose I should make somethin' up. Satisfy everybody. It's good for business. But I'm near wore out."

Having worked for him, Fletch knew Walter March had massages frequently. Apparently at least eight other reporters knew that too.

"If you want a massage, I'll give you a massage." She took her hands off him, and looked up and down his body. "If you want me to talk, I'll talk. I'll just charge you for the massage. Either way."

Fletch looked into a corner of the ceiling.

He said, "I tip."

"Okay."

Her fingers went into his leg again.

"Your body don't look like the other reporters'."

Fletch said, "Walter March."

"He had a good body. Very good body for an old gentleman. Slim. Good skin tone, you know what I mean?"

"You mean you massaged him?"

"Sure."

"Not the masseur?"

"What's surprising about that? I'm rubbing you."

"Walter March was sort of puritanical."

"What's that got to do with it?"

She was working her way up his left leg.

Fletch said, "Oh, boy."

"That feel good?"

Fletch said, "Life is hard."

"Walter March was a pretty important man?"

"Yes."

"He ran a newspaper or something?"

"He owned a lot of them."

"He was very courteous," she said. "Courtly. Tipped good."

"I've got it about the tip," Fletch said.

She finished his left arm.

Suspending her breasts over his face, she rubbed his stomach and chest muscles vigorously.

"Oh, God," he said.

"What?"

"These are not ideal working conditions."

"I'm the one who's doing the work. Turn over."

Face down, nose in the massage table's nose hole, Fletch said, "Walter March." He couldn't get himself up to asking specific questions in a sequence. He blew the bunched-up sheet away from his mouth. "Tell me what you told the eight other reporters."

"I didn't tell them much. Not much to tell."

She lifted his lower left leg and, with a tight grip, was running her hand up his calf muscle.

"Oi," he said.

"Are you Jewish?"

"Everyone who's being tortured is Jewish."

"Mister March said nice day, he said he loved being in Virginia, he said they'd had nice weather the last few days in Washington, too, he said he wanted a firm rub, like you, with oil. . . ."

"Not so firm," Fletch said. She was doing the same thing to his right calf muscles. "Not so firm."

"He asked if I was Swedish, I said I came from Pittsburgh, he asked how come I had become a masseuse, I said my mother taught me, she came from Newfoundland, he asked me what my husband does for a living, I said he works for the town water department, how many kids I have, how many people I massage a day on the average, weekdays and weekends, he asked me the population of the town of Hendricks and if I knew anything about the original Hendricks family. You know. We just talked."

Fletch was always surprised when publishers performed automatically and instinctively as reporters.

Old Walter March had gotten a hell of a lot of basic information—background material—out of the "little old lady rubbing bones in the basement."

And, Fletch knew, March had done it for no particular reason, other than to orient himself.

Fletch would be doing the same thing, if he could keep his brain muscles taut while someone was loosening his leg muscles.

She put her fists into his ass cheeks, and rotated them vigorously. Then she kneaded them with her thumbs.

"Oof, oof," Fletch said.

"You've even got muscle there," she said.

"So I'm discovering."

She began to work on his back.

"You should be rubbed more often," she said. "Keep you loose. Relaxed."

"I've got better ways of keeping loose."

He found himself breathing more deeply, evenly.

Her thumbs were working up his spinal column.

He gave in to the back rub. He had little choice.

Finally, when she was done, he sat on the edge of the table. His head swayed.

She was washing the oil off her hands.

"Was Walter March nervous?" he asked. "Did he seem upset, in any way, afraid of anything? Anxious?"

"No." She was drying her hands on a towel. "But he should have been."

"Obviously."

"That's not what I mean. I had a reporter in here earlier today. I think he could have killed Walter March."

"What do you mean?"

"He kept swearing at him. Calling him dirty names.

54

Instead of asking about Mister March, the way the rest of you did, he kept calling him that so-and-so. Only he didn't say so-and-so."

"What was his name?"

"I don't know. I suppose I could look up the charge slip. He was a big man, fortyish, heavy, sideburns and mustache. A Northerner. A real angry person. You know, one of those people who are always angry. Big sense of injustice."

"Oh."

"And then there was the man in the parking lot yesterday."

She put her towel neatly on the rack over the wash basin.

"When I drove in yesterday morning, he was walking across the parking lot. He came over to me. He asked if I worked here. I thought he was someone looking for a job, you know? He was dressed that way, blue jeans jacket. Tight, curly gray hair although he wasn't old, skinny body—like the guys who work down at the stables, you know? A horse person. He asked if Walter March had arrived yet. First I'd ever heard of Walter March. His eyes were bloodshot. His jaw muscles were the tightest muscles I'd ever seen."

"What did you do?"

"I got away from him."

Fletch looked at the big, muscular blond woman.

"You mean he frightened you?"

She said, "Yes."

"Did you tell the other reporters about him?"

"No." She said, "I guess it takes nine times being asked the same questions, for me to have remembered him."

Eight

AMERICAN JOURNALISM ALLIANCE
Walter March, President

SCHEDULE OF EVENTS
Hendricks Plantation
Hendricks, Virginia

Monday
6:30 P.M. Welcoming Cocktail Party
   Amanda Hendricks Room

"Hi," Fletch said cheerfully. He had stuck his head around the corner of the hotel's switchboard.

Behind him, across the lobby, people were gathering in the Amanda Hendricks Room.

The telephone operator nearer him said, "You're not supposed to be in here, sir."

Both operators looked as startled as rabbits caught in a flashlight beam.

"I'm just here to pick up the sheet," he said.

"What sheet?"

He popped his eyes.

"The survey sheet. You're supposed to have it for me."

The further operator had gone back to working the switchboard.

"The sheet for us to take the surveys."

56

"Helen, do you know anything about a survey sheet?"

The other operator said, "Hendricks Plantation. Good evening."

"You know," Fletch said. "From Information. The sheet that says who's in which room. Names and room numbers. For us to take the surveys."

"Oh," the girl said.

She looked worriedly at the sheet clipped onto the board in front of her.

"Yeah," Fletch squinted at it. "That's the one."

"But that's mine," she said.

"But you're supposed to have one for me," he said.

She said, "Helen, do we have another one of these sheets?"

Helen said, "I'm sorry, sir. That room does not answer."

Fletch said, "She has another one."

"But I need mine," the girl said.

"You can Xerox hers."

"We can't leave the switchboard. It's much too busy."

She connected with a flashing light. "Hendricks Plantation. Good evening."

"Give me yours," Fletch said. Helpfully, he slipped it out of its clip. "I'll Xerox it."

"I think the office is locked," she whispered. "I'll ring, sir."

"All you have to do is move Helen's." He reached over and put Helen's information sheet between them. "And you can both see it."

The operator said, "I'm sorry, sir, but a cocktail reception is going on here, and I don't think many people are in their rooms."

Helen scowled angrily at him, as she said, "The dining room is open for breakfast at seven o'clock, sir."

"Tell me." Fletch was looking at the sheet in his hands. "Lydia March and Walter March, Junior, aren't still in the suite Walter March died in this morning, are they?"

"No," the operator said. "They've been moved to Suite 12."

"Thanks." Fletch waved the telephone information sheet at them. " 'Preciate it."

Nine

Fletch had saw-toothed seven edges of two credit cards letting himself into over twenty rooms and suites at Hendricks Plantation before he got caught.

He had just placed bug Number 22 to the back of the bedside lamp in Room 42 and was recrossing the room when he heard a key scratching on the outside of the lock.

He turned immediately for the bathroom, but then heard the lock click.

An apparent burglar, he stood in the middle of Room 42, pretending to be deeply concerned with the telephone information sheet, wondering how he could use it to give some official explanation for his presence in someone else's room.

Next to each room number and occupant's name was the number of the bug he had planted in the room.

The door handle was turning.

"Ahem," he said to himself. No official frame of mind was occurring to him.

"Ahem."

The door was being pushed open unnaturally slowly.

In the door, swaying, breathing shallowly, thin red hair splaying up from her head, an aquamarine evening

59

gown lopsided on her, was the great White House wire
service reporter, Leona Hatch.

Watery, glazed eyes took a moment to focus on him.
Her right shoulder lurched against the door jamb.

"Oh," she said to the apparent burglar. "Thank God
you're here."

And she began to fall.

Fletch grabbed her before she hit the floor.

Dead-weight. She was totally unconscious. She reeked
of booze.

Gently, he put her head on the floor.

"Zowie."

He turned down her bed before carrying her to it
and putting her neatly on it.

He put on the bedside lamp.

She was wearing a tight necklace—a choker he
thought might choke her—so he lifted her head and
felt around in the seventy-odd-years-old woman's thin
hair until he found the clasp. He left the necklace on
her bedside table.

He took off her shoes.

Looking at her, he wondered what else he could do
to loosen her clothes, and realized she was wearing a
corset. His fingers confirmed it.

"Oh, hell."

He rolled her onto her side to get at the zipper in
the back of her gown.

"Errrrrrr," Leona Hatch said. "Errrrrrrrrr."

"Don't throw up," he answered, with great sincerity.

Pulling her gown off her from the bottom, he had to
keep returning to the head of the bed and pulling her
up toward the pillows by the shoulders. Or, before the
gown was off her, she would have been on the floor.

He tossed the gown over a side chair, and realized
he had to repeat the process with a slip.

The corset took great study.

In his travels, Fletch had never come across a corset.

In fact, he had never come across so many clothes on one person before.

"Oh, well," he said. "I suppose you'd do it for me."

"Errrrrrrrr," she protested every time he revolved her to get her corset off. "Errrrrrrrr!"

"How do I know? Maybe you already have."

Finally he left her in what he supposed was the last level of underclothes, loosened as much as he could manage, and flipped the sheet and blanket over her.

"Good night, sweet Princess." He turned out the bedside lamp. "Dream sweet dreams, and, when you awake, think kindly on the Bumptious Bandit! 'Daughter, did you hear hoofbeats in the night?' " He left a light on across the room, to orient her when she awoke. " 'Father, Father, I thought it were the palpitations of my own heart!' "

Letting himself out, the telephone information sheet firmly in hand, Fletch said, " 'It were, Daughter. Booze does that to you.' "

Ten

9:00 P.M. Welcoming Remarks
TERRORISM AND TELEVISION
Address by Hy Litwack

"I was afraid you'd show up," Bob McConnell said.

Dinner was half over when Fletch arrived to take his assigned seat, at a corner table for six.

McConnell—a big man, fortyish, heavy, with sideburns and a mustache—had been alone at the table with Crystal Faoni and Fredericka Arbuthnot.

"I knew a table for six, empty except for two girls and myself, was too good to last."

"Hi, Bob."

"Hi."

"They put us together," Fredericka Arbuthnot said to Fletch. "Isn't that chummy?"

"Chummy."

Fletch glanced at the considerable distance to the head table.

"I guess none of us is considered too important," he said. "Another few feet to the right, through that wall, and we could stack our dishes in the dishwasher without leaving the table."

Bob said, "Yeah."

A few years before, Robert McConnell had left his job at a newspaper and spent ten months as press aide to a presidential candidate.

It would have been the chance of a lifetime.

Except the candidate lost.

His newspaper had taken him back, of course, but begrudgingly, and at the same old job.

His publisher, Walter March, had considered his mistaken judgment more important than his gained experience.

Walter March's judgment hadn't been wrong.

He had had his newspapers endorse the other candidate—who had won.

And it had taken Robert McConnell the interim years to work himself out of both the emotional and financial depression taking such a chance had caused.

Crystal said, "How was your massage, sybarite?"

Bob said, "You had a massage?"

To a good reporter, everything was significant.

"I was sleepy, afterwards," Fletch said.

"I should take massages," Crystal said. "Maybe it would help me get rid of some of this fat."

"Crystal, darling," Fletch said. "You're a bore."

"Me?"

"All you do is talk about your fat."

Because he was late, the waiter placed in front of Fletch—all at one time—the fruit cup, salad, roast beef, potato, peas, cake with strawberry goo poured over the top, and coffee.

"You want a drink?" the waiter asked.

Fletch said, "I guess not."

"My fat is all anybody ever talks about," Crystal said.

"Only in response to your incessant comments about it." Fletch chewed the pale slices of grapefruit and orange from the fruit cup. "Historic Hendricks Plantation," he said. "Even their fruit cup is antebellum."

"I never, never mention my fat," Crystal said.

Purposely, humorously, she began to fork his salad.

"You never talk about anything else." Fletch pulled his roast beef out of her range. "You're like one of these people with a dog or a horse or a boat or a garden or something who never talk about anything but their damn dog, horse, boat, or, what else did I say?"

"Garden," said Freddie.

"Garden," said Fletch. "Boring, boring, boring."

Crystal was sopping up the salad dressing with a piece of bread. "It must be defensive."

"Stupid," Fletch said. "You have nothing to be defensive about."

"I'm fat."

"You've got beautiful skin."

"Meters and meters of it."

She reached for his dessert.

Fredericka Arbuthnot said to Robert McConnell, "This is I. M. Fletcher. He gets along well with everybody."

"This stupid American idea," Fletch said, "that everybody has to look emaciated."

Crystal's voice was muffled through the strawberry-goo-topped cake. "Look who's talking. You're not fat."

"Inside every slim person," Fletch proclaimed, "is a fat person trying to get out."

"Yeah," muttered Freddie. "But through the mouth?"

"If you'd stop telling people you're fat," Fletch declaimed, "no one would notice!"

Her mouth still full of cake, Crystal looked sideways at Fletch.

She could contain herself no longer.

She and Fletch both began to laugh and choke and laugh and laugh.

With her left hand Crystal was holding her side. With her right, she was holding her napkin to her face.

Not laughing, Fredericka Arbuthnot and Robert McConnell were watching them.

Crystal began to reach for his coffee.

Fletch banged her wrist onto the table.

"Leave the coffee!"

Crystal nearly rolled out of her chair—laughing.

Robert McConnell had signaled the waiter.

"Bring drinks, all around, will you? We need to catch up with these two."

The waiter scanned the dead glasses on the table, and looked inquiringly at Fletch.

Bob said, "Fletch?"

"I don't care."

"Bring him a brandy," Bob said. "He needs a steadier."

"Bring him another dessert," Crystal said. "I need it!"

Fletch sat back from his plate.

"Oh, I can't eat any more. I've laughed too hard." He looked at Crystal. "You want it, Crystal?"

"Sure," she said.

The plate stayed in front of Fletch.

Freddie asked Fletch, "Who were you talking to in your room?"

"Talking to?"

"I couldn't help hearing you through the wall."

"Hearing me through the wall?"

"It sounded like you were practicing a speech."

"Practicing a speech?"

"I couldn't hear any other voice."

"I was talking to Crystal," Fletch said. "On the phone."

"No," Freddie shook her head. "It sounded recorded. At one point, when I first heard you, you blurted out something. As if the playback volume was too high."

"Oh, yeah. I was using a tape recorder. Few notes to myself."

"A few notes on what?" Bob sat up straight so the waiter could set the drink in front of him.

"Ah, ha!" Crystal said. "The great investigative reporter, Irwin Maurice Fletcher, has discovered who killed Walter March!"

"Actually," Fletch said. "I have."

"Who?" Freddie said.

Fletch said, "Robert McConnell."

Across the table, Bob's eyes narrowed.

Freddie looked at Bob. "Motive?"

"For having his newspapers endorse the opposition," Fletch said, "a few years back. It snatched the candy apple right out of Bob's mouth. Didn't it, Bob?" Robert McConnell's face had gone slightly pale. "If March's newspapers hadn't endorsed the opposition, Bob's man probably would have won. Bob would have gone to the White House. Instead, he ended up back at the same old metal desk in the City Room, facing a blank wall, with thousands of dollars of personal bank loans outstanding."

Fletch and Bob were staring at each other across the table, Fletch with a small smile.

Freddie was looking from one to the other.

"A few notes on what?" Bob asked.

Fletch shrugged. "A travel piece. I've been in Italy. By the way, has anyone seen Junior?"

Walter March, Junior, was the sort, at fifty, people continued to call "Junior."

"I hear he's drinking," Crystal said.

"Jake Williams took him and Lydia for a car ride." Bob sat back in his chair, relaxed his shoulders. "He wanted to get them out of here. Get Junior some air."

Freddie said, "You mean the police are making Mrs. March and son stay at this damned convention, where Walter March was murdered? How cruel."

"I suspect they could do something about it," Bob said, "if they want to."

Crystal said, "When you have the power of March Newspapers behind you, you are apt to be very, very conciliatory to petty authority."

"At least, openly," Bob said.

"At least, initially," Fletch said.

"Oh, come on," said the lady who had said she was from *Newsworld* magazine, but didn't appear to know very much. "Newspaper chains aren't very powerful, these days."

The three newspaper reporters looked at each other.

"March Newspapers?" Crystal Faoni said.

"Pretty powerful," Robert McConnell said.

"Yeah," Fletch said. "They even publish other months of the year."

There was the tinkle of spoon against glass from the head table.

"Here it comes," Bob McConnell said. "The after-dinner regurgitation. Duck."

Fletch turned his chair, to face the dais.

"Anybody got a cigar?" Bob asked. "I've always wanted to blow smoke up Hy Litwack's nose."

Helena Williams was standing at the dais.

"Does this thing work?" she asked the microphone.

Her amplified voice bounced off the walls.

"No!" said the audience.

"Of course not!" said the audience.

"Ask it again, Helena!" said the audience.

"Good evening," said Helena, in her best modulated voice.

The audience stopped scraping its chairs and began restraining its smoke-coughs.

"Despite the tragic circumstances of the death of the president of the American Journalism Alliance's president, Walter March"—she stopped, flustered, took a deep breath, and, in the best game-old-girl tradition, continued—"it is a pleasure to see you all, and to welcome you to the Forty-Ninth Annual Meeting of the American Journalism Alliance's Convention.

"Walter March was to make a welcoming speech at this point, but. . . ."

"But," Robert McConnell said, softly, "old Walter's being sent home in a box."

". . . Well," Helena said, "of course there is no one who can stand in his place.

"Instead, let us recognize all that Walter has done, both for the Alliance, and, for each of us, individually as newspeople, over the years. . . ."

"Yeah," said Robert McConnell.

"Yeah," said Crystal Faoni.

". . . and join in a moment of silence."

"Hey, Fletch," Bob said in a stage whisper, "got a deck of cards?"

There was a moment of quiet muttering.

Across the room, Tim Shields was waving at a waiter to bring him a drink.

"I'm sure it has nothing to do with the tragic circumstances," Helena said, "but the after-dinner speech scheduled for Wednesday evening by the President of the United States has been canceled. . . ."

"Oh, shucks." Bob looked at Fletch. "And here I brought two pairs of scissors."

". . . However, the Vice-President has arranged to come."

"The Administration has decided not to ignore us completely," Crystal Faoni said, "just because we've taken to stabbing each other in the back more openly than usual."

"Just one other announcement," Helena said, "before I introduce Hy Litwack. Well, why don't I just introduce Virginia State Police Captain Andrew Neale, who has been placed in charge of poor Walter's. . . ."

Helena stepped away from the microphone.

A man with salt and pepper short hair, a proper military bearing in a tweed jacket, stood up from a table near the main door and walked to the dais. Clearly, he had not expected to be called upon.

Bob McConnell said, "I betcha he says, 'Last, but not least.' "

With poise, but blushing slightly, Captain Neale addressed the microphone.

"Good evening," he said, in a soft, deep drawl. "Accept my sympathy for the loss of the president of your association."

"Accepted," Bob muttered. "Easily accepted."

"First," Captain Neale said, "I've asked that your convention not be canceled. I'm sure that the death of Walter March casts a tragic pall over your meetings. . . ."

"An appalling pall," said Bob.

". . . but I trust you all will be able to go about your business with as little interference as possible from me and the people working with me.

"Second, of course we will have to take statements from those of you who were actually here at Hendricks Plantation this morning at the time of the tragic occurrence. Your cooperation in being available to us, and open with us, will be greatly appreciated.

"Third, I realize that I am surrounded here by some of the world's greatest reporters. Frankly, I feel like Daniel in the den of lions. I understand that each of you feels the necessity of reporting the story of Walter March's murder to your newspapers or networks, and I will try to be as fair with you as I can. But please understand that I, too, have to do my job. Many of you have already come to me with questions. If I do nothing but answer your questions, I won't be doing my job, which is to investigate this tragedy, and, there won't be any answers. As solid facts are developed, I will see that you get them. It would help if there were no rumor or speculation."

"Here it comes," Bob said.

Captain Neale said, "Last, but not least, if any of you have genuine information which might help in this investigation, of course we will appreciate your reporting that information to me or one of the people working with me.

"Someone at Hendricks Plantation murdered Walter March this morning, with premeditation. No one has been allowed to leave the plantation since this morning. Someone here—most likely in this room—is guilty of first degree murder.

"I will appreciate your cooperation in every way."

Captain Neale started from the microphone, bent back to it, and said, "Thank you."

"Good old boy," said Bob. "Good cop."

"Bright and decent," said Crystal.

Freddie Arbuthnot said, "Ineffectual."

Helena said Hy Litwack needed no introduction, and so she gave him none.

Bob McConnell said, "I bet he says, 'Don't shoot the messenger.' "

Crystal and Fletch shrugged at each other.

Hy Litwack, anchorman for evening network news, was highly respected by everyone except other journalists, most of whom were purely envious of him.

He was handsome, dignified, with a grand voice, solid manner, and had been earning a fabulous annual income for many years. He was staffed like no journalist in history had ever been staffed.

An additional point of envy was that he was also an incredibly good journalist.

Unlike many another television newsman, he kept his showmanship to a minimum.

And, unlike many other journalists of roughly comparable power and prestige, there was minimal evidence of bias in his reporting—even in the questions he asked in live interview situations. He never led his audience, or anyone he was interviewing.

Also enviable was his on-camera stamina, through conventions, elections, and other continuous-coverage stories.

Hy Litwack had been at the top of the heap for years.

Next to him at the head table sat his wife, Carol.

"Good evening." The famous voice cleared his throat. "When I have an opportunity to speak, I try to speak on the topics I find people most frequently ask me about, whether I wish to speak about them or not.

"Recently, people have been asking me most about acts of terrorism, more specifically about television news coverage of acts of terrorism, most specifically whether by covering terrorism, television news is encouraging, or even causing, other terrorists to implement their dreadful, frequently insane fantasies.

"I hate witnessing terrorism. I hate reading about it. I hate reporting it—as I'm sure we all do.

"But television did not create terrorism.

"Terrorism, like many another crime or insanity, is infectious. It perpetuates itself. It causes itself to happen. One incident of terrorism causes two more incidents, which cause more and more and more incidents.

"Never was this social phenomenon, of acts of terrorism stimulating other acts of terrorism, on and on, more apparent than at the beginning of the twentieth century.

"And television, or television news, at that point had not yet even been dreamed of.

"An act of terrorism is an event. It is news.

"And it is our job to bring the news to the people, whether we personally like that news, or not."

Bob McConnell whispered, "Here it comes."

"Blaming television," Hy Litwack continued, "for causing acts of terrorism simply by reporting them is as bad as shooting the messenger simply because the news he brings is bad. . . ."

Eleven

In the privacy of their bedroom, Carol Litwack was saying to her husband, ". . . Live to be a hundred, I'll never get over it."

"Over what?"

"You. I don't know."

At a distance there was the sound of gargling.

Before leaving for dinner, Fletch had tuned the receiver to Leona Hatch's room, Room 42, so he could check on her later, make sure she was as comfortable as possible. All he had expected to hear on the tape was snoring and "Errrrrrrr's."

But that wasn't the way the marvelous machine worked.

Like all things governmental, it had its own system of priorities.

It took him a while to figure it out.

First he heard Leona Hatch snoring in Room 42, on Station 22, then Station 21 lit and he heard Sheldon Levi's toilet flushing in Room 48, then Station 4 lit and he heard Eleanor Earles saying in Suite 9, ". . . Dressed to hear Hy Litwack's stupid speech. Ugh! But if I don't, I suppose there'll be three pages in *TV Guide* about my snubbing the pan-fried son of a bitch at the American Journalism . . ." and then Station 2 lit and he heard Carol and Hy Litwack talking in Suite 5.

Any noise in any room in which he had placed a

lower-numbered bug had precedence over any noise in any room in which he had placed a higher-numbered bug.

Fletch studied his telephone information sheet, and the notes he had made on it regarding which bugs he had put where, and discovered he had placed bugs instinctively more or less in accordance with the machine's priorities.

To keep himself straight at what he was doing, and, in fear of eventually being caught as he let himself into other people's rooms, he had planted the lower-numbered bugs in the rooms of the more important people: Station 1 was Suite 12, Lydia March and Walter March, Junior; Station 2, the Litwacks, in Suite 5; Station 3, Helena and Jake Williams, in Suite 7; Station 4, Eleanor Earles, in Suite 9. In Suite 3, now empty—it being where Walter March had been murdered—he had placed bug Number 5. And, in Room 77, Fredericka Arbuthnot's, he had placed bug Number 23.

"My, my," Fletch said of his marvelous machine, "it walks, it talks, cries 'Mama!' and piddles genuine orange juice!"

Hy Litwack spent a long time gargling his famous throat—every bubble and blurp of which Fletch faithfully recorded.

Carol Litwack was saying, "Here you are, the most successful, respected journalist in the country, in the whole world, a multimillionaire on top of that, and you still feel you can't say what you want to say, what you think is the truth."

"Like what?" Hy Litwack's voice sounded tired and bored.

"Well, what you just said about terrorism and television downstairs is not what you've said to me about terrorism and television."

Clearly, Hy Litwack was having a bedtime conversation with his wife which did not interest him much. "I mentioned the possibility that the more publicity we give terrorists and murderers the more other kooks are apt to commit acts of terror and murder for the publicity alone. Too many people want to be on television, even with a gun in hand, or in handcuffs, or lying face down in the street with their backs riddled with police bullets . . . how much more of my speech would you like me to repeat to you? I admitted all that. I said I worry about it. But I don't know what to do about it. No one does. News is news, and it's seldom good."

There was a feminine sigh. "That's not what you've said to me at all."

"What have I said different?"

"Hy, you know you have. Time after time you've said to me the networks give maximum exposure to acts of terrorism in progress because it gets the ratings up."

Hy Litwack said, "They make for good drama."

"People tune in, especially, to see if the hostages or whoever have gotten machine-gunned yet. Or had their heads chopped off. You know you've said this."

"Yes," Hy Litwack said. "I've said this. To you."

"You didn't say it tonight. In your speech. An ongoing act of terrorism and the whole network news department comes alive. You rush to the studio, day or night. People switch on their TV sets. Audience ratings go up."

"I said they make for good drama."

"The advertisers' commercials get more exposure," Carol said. "Here some little nut out in Chicago, or Cleveland, is holding twenty people hostage to protest the establishment in some way, and in boardrooms all across the country the establishment is cheering because the poor little nut is helping to sell the establishment's products to all the other nuts and thus make the establishment richer!"

"Everything makes the establishment richer."

"You've said that. To me. Why didn't you say it in your speech tonight? Are you so establishment yourself you can't say what you really think, as a journalist?"

"No," said Hy Litwack. "But I'm a good enough journalist to keep my cynicism to myself."

There was what seemed to Fletch a long silence. He was waiting to hear where the marvelous machine would switch next.

He was about to experiment, to see if he could run the machine manually, when he again heard Carol Litwack's voice. "Oh, Hy. You don't know what I'm talking about."

"I guess not," said the famous voice, now sleepy.

"This afternoon you rushed down here to Virginia early, and immediately taped that phony eulogy on Walter March for the network evening news. 'The great journalist, Walter March of March Newspapers, is dead,' you intoned, 'shockingly murdered at the convention of the American Journalism Alliance, of which March was the elected president.'"

"I never said 'shockingly murdered.'"

"You even put on your tight-throat bit."

"You can check the tape."

"Whatever you said."

"Whatever I said."

"You didn't even know Walter March. Really."

"No man is an island."

"The few times you met him you told me the same thing about him. He was a cold fish."

"Carol? Would you mind if we went to sleep now?"

"You're not listening."

"No. I'm not."

"Just because all you famous newspeople are here,

76

because it's a cheap story, cheap drama, because you're competing with each other between martinis, you're giving Walter March's murder more publicity than World War Two!"

"Carol!"

The famous voice was no longer sleepy. It sounded as if someone had just declared World War Three.

"You still don't know what I'm saying."

"Do I have to sleep in the living room?"

"You don't know what you're doing," Carol said. "You can't."

"Carol. . . ."

"Giving March's murder all this publicity—all you're doing is inciting some other kook—maybe hundreds of publicity-hungry kooks—to see if they can stick a knife, or scissors, or whatever, into the back of some other quote great American journalist unquote."

"Carol, for God's sake!"

There was another long silence.

Then Carol Litwack's voice said, "I just hope the next quote great American journalist unquote murdered isn't you."

Fletch switched to Station 22, and heard only one "Errrrrrr" in three minutes of snores.

He discovered that if he depressed a station button, and shoved it up a little, it would catch and remain on that station.

On Station 23 he heard the shower running and Fredericka Arbuthnot singing a little ditty that apparently went, "Hoo, boy, now I wash my left knee; Hoo, boy, now I wash my right knee. . . ."

Fletch said, "Hoo, boy. Nice knees. Treacherous heart."

Fletch scanned the other stations.

There was conversation on Station 8, in syndicated humorist Oscar Perlman's suite.

". . . like this and five dollars and you couldn't even get a good dollar cigar."

"There's a good dollar cigar now?"

"I'm in. Two."

"Three little words. Make 'em nice."

"Nice? One, two, three. Those are nice?"

"You're asking? You dealt 'em."

"I deal without prejudice."

". . . Litwack."

Oscar Perlman had written a play and a few books and had been on television often and his was the only voice Fletch recognized.

Listening, Fletch could not even be sure how many men were in the room.

He presumed they were all Washington newspapermen.

"Fuckin' phony."

"Who's talking about Litwack?"

"You recognized the description? I'm out."

"He's just good-lookin'," said Perlman.

"He's no journalist. He's just an actor."

"All us plug-uglies are jealous of him," said Perlman, " 'cause he's good-lookin'."

"He's no actor, either. Anybody see him jerking himself off over March's death on the evening ersatz news show?"

"Ersatz? Wha's'at, ersatz?"

" 'There's no business, like show business,' that's news. . . ."

"How much of Litwack's income comes from his face, Walter?"

"His face and his voice? Thirty percent."

"Ninety percent, Oscar. Ninety percent."

"He looks like everybody's father. As last seen. Laid out in the coffin."

"Whose deal?"

"Something all you guys are too jealous to recognize," said Oscar Perlman, "is that Hy Litwack is a good journalist."

"A good journalist?"

"Don't bother. I'm folding right now. Your dealing has driven me to drink."

"Shit."

"Oscar, I thought I saw you sitting downstairs listening to Hy Litwack's speech. In fact, I thought I saw you sitting next to me?"

"I was there."

"You heard that speech and still tell us you think Hy Litwack is a good, honest, no-bullshit journalist?"

Someone else said, "That speech was written for some afternoon ladies' society out in Ohio. Not for his colleagues, Oscar."

"That's true. Hit me once, and hit me twice, and hit me once again, it's been a long, long time."

"Fuckin' superior bastard."

"So?" Oscar Perlman said. "He's not the first speaker who misjudged his audience. What are you going to do, wrap a coaxial cable around his neck and turn on the juice?"

"At least he might have asked one of his three thousand staff members to write a new speech for us."

"Another reason you're all jealous of him," said Oscar Perlman, "is because Hy Litwack has a big, six-figure income."

There was a momentary silence.

Someone said, quietly, "So have you, Oscar."

"Yeah. But you bastards have figured out a way of taking it away from me—over the poker table."

There was a laugh.

"Oscar's defending Hy because they're both establishment. The two richest men in journalism."

"That's right," said Oscar. "Only Litwack's smarter than I am. He doesn't play poker."

"You going to do a column on Walter March's death, Oscar?"

"I don't see anything funny about getting a pair of scissors up the ass. Even I can't make anything funny out of that."

"You can't?"

"Pair of deuces. Pair of rockets."

"And the devils are up and away, Five-Card Charlie."

"No," said Oscar Perlman. "I can't."

"How much money has Walter March cost you, Oscar?"

"It's not the money. It's the grief."

"Sizable bill. First, when you were working for him in Washington, for years March refused to syndicate you. He wouldn't even let your column run in other March newspapers."

"He said what was funny in Washington no one would think funny in Dallas. He was wrong about Dallas."

"Then when the syndicate picked you up, he sued you, saying you had developed the column while working on his newspaper, and he had the original copyright."

"No one ever got rich working for Walter March."

"How much did all that cost you, Oscar?"

"Nothing."

"Nothing?"

"You can't sue talent."

"You didn't buy him off?"

"Of course not."

"Legal fees?"

"There were some."

80

"Grief?"

"A lot. I'll never forgive him. Frankly, I'll never forgive him. Never."

"Then immediately he started nudging, saying if your column was going to run, it had to run in his newspapers. Right?"

"The bastard threatened about every contract I've had with every newspaper in this country."

"This has been going on for years and years. Right, Oscar?"

"What are you doing, playing cards or working on a story?"

"I don't get it," another voice said. "So Walter March has been biting your tail all these years. Why all the grief? Lawyers are for grief. You can't afford lawyers, Oscar?"

"You don't know how Walter March operated?"

"Look at that. Nine, ten, Queen."

"Tell me."

"If you don't know how Walter March operated, you never worked for him."

"Yeah, I only need one."

"A little blackmail. Always a little blackmail."

Someone else said, "That son of a bitch had more private eyes on his payroll than he had reporters. Paid 'em better, too."

"And they didn't have to write."

"A cute man. Real cute."

"Shit. Son of a bitch. I'm out."

"You mean Walter March has been blackmailing you, Oscar?"

"No. Just trying to find a way to. Pair of eyes behind every bush. I'm flying first class—there's always the same son of a bitch flying coach. No matter what city I'm in, there's always someone waiting for me in the hotel lobby to see if I go up in the elevator alone. Nuisance value, you know?"

"Dear old saintly Walter March operated like that?"

"Dear old saintly Walter March. The president of your American Journalism Alliance. You voted for him? Give me one card, so long as it's the King of Clubs."

"I'm very grateful to him," said Oscar Perlman. "Kept me straight all these years. I've never had the opportunity to lie to my wife."

"Oscar, you don't think dear old saintly Walter March getting a scissors up the ass is funny?"

Oscar Perlman said, "Not worth a column."

"I take it we're not sleeping together?"

Fletch said into the phone, "Who is this?"

It was 1:20 A.M. He had been asleep a half-hour.

"Damn you!" said Freddie Arbuthnot. "Damn your eyes, your nose, and, your cock!"

The phone went dead.

It wasn't that Fletch hadn't thought of it.

He knew she'd washed her knees.

Twelve

And in the morning, the phone was ringing as he entered his room.

He took off his sweaty T-shirt before answering.

"Have you seen the papers?" Crystal asked.

"No. I went for a ride."

"Ride? You're unemployed and you rented a car?"

"I'm unemployed and I rented a horse. They use less gas."

"A horse! You mean one of those big things with four legs who eat hay?"

"That's a cow," Fletch said.

"Or a horse."

It took Crystal a moment more of exclamations before accepting the idea that someone would get up before dawn, find the stables in the dark, rent a horse, and ride over the hills eastward watching the sun rise, "without a thought for breakfast."

It had been a pleasant horse and a great sunrise.

And taking the horse from the stables and bringing it back, Fletch had not seen the man in the blue denim jacket, with tight, curly gray hair, who had approached the masseuse, Mrs. Leary, in the parking lot two morn-

83

ings before and asked her about the arrival of Walter March.

"I want to read you just one 'graf from Bob McConnell's story in March's Washington newspaper regarding the old bastard's murder."

"Pretty extensive coverage?"

"Pages and pages. Two pages just of photographs, going back to and including a shot of the bastard at the baptismal font."

"He deserves every line," said Fletch. "Dear old saintly Walter March."

"Anyway, Bob nailed you."

"Yeah?"

"I'll just read the paragraph. First he names all the big names here at the convention. Then he writes, 'Also attending the convention is Irwin Maurice Fletcher, who, although never indicted, previously has figured prominently in murder trials in the states of California and Massachusetts. Currently unemployed, Fletcher has worked for a March newspaper.' "

Fletch was pulling off his jeans.

He had listened to McConnell phoning in his story the night before.

"A pretty heavy tat for tit, Fletcher. Methinks you'll not jokingly accuse Bob McConnell of first-degree murder again. At least, not in his presence."

"Who was joking?"

"There are some pretty vicious people around here," Crystal said.

"You didn't know?"

"Breakfast?"

"Got to shower first."

"Please do."

84

Thirteen

9:30 A.M.

IS GOD DEAD, OR JUST DE-PRESSED?
Address by Rt. Rev. James Halford
Conservatory

10:00 A.M.

IS ANYONE OUT THERE?
Weekly Newspapers Group Discussion
Bobby-Joe Hendricks Cocktail Lounge

Fletch had breakfast in his room, listening to Virginia State Police Captain Andrew Neale questioning Lydia March and Walter March, Junior, in Suite 12.

There were the preliminary courtesies—Captain Neale saying, "I know this must be terribly difficult for you, Mrs. March"; Lydia saying, "I know it's necessary"; his saying, "Thank you. You have my sympathy. I would avoid disturbing you at this point if it were at all possible"—while Fletch was spooning his half a grapefruit.

Junior had to be fetched from his bedroom.

"Junior's a little slow this morning," Lydia said. "Neither of us is getting any sleep, of course."

"Hello, Mister Neale," Junior said.

His voice was not as clear as Lydia's or Neale's.

"Good morning, Mister March. I've told your mother that you have my sympathy, and I hate to put you both through this. . . ."

"Right," Junior said. "Hate to go through it. Hate to go through the whole shabby thing."

"If you would just go over the circumstances of your husband's. . . . You don't mind my using a tape recorder, do you?"

Junior said, "Tape recorder?"

"Of course not, Captain Neale. Do anything you like."

"As an aid to my memory, and hopefully, so I won't have to disturb you again. It's most important that we fix the timing of this . . . incident precisely."

"Incident!" said Junior.

"Sorry," said Neale. "All words are inadequate. . . ."

"Apparently," said Junior.

"We're particularly interested in. . . ."

"I'll do my best, Captain," Lydia said. "Only it's so. . . ."

"Mrs. March, if you can just describe everything, every detail, from the moment you woke up yesterday morning?"

"Yes. Well, we, that is, Walter and I, were scheduled to have breakfast at eight o'clock yesterday morning with Helena and Jake Williams—Helena is the Executive Secretary of the Alliance—to go over everything a final time before the mobs arrived, you know, discuss any problems there might have been. . . ."

"Were there any you knew of?"

"Any what?"

"Any problems."

"No. Not really. There was a small problem about the President."

"The president of what?"

". . . the United States."

"Oh. What was that?"

"What was what?"

"The problem with the President of the United States."

"Oh. Well, you see, he doesn't play golf."

"I know."

"Well, you see, he was scheduled to arrive at three in the afternoon. By helicopter. The problem was what to do with him until dinner. Presidents of the United States have always played golf. Almost always. At these conventions, the President goes out and walks around the golf course with a few members of the press, and it makes good picture opportunities for the working press, and it makes it seem to the public that we're doing something for him, helping him to relax, giving him a break from work, and that the press and the President can be friendly, you know. . . ."

"I see."

"But the President, this President, doesn't play golf. The night before, Jake—that's Mister Williams—over drinks—well, we were talking about this and Jake was making silly suggestions, of what to do with the President of the United States for four hours. He suggested we fill up the swimming pool with catfish and give the President a net and let him wade in and catch them all. I shouldn't be saying this. Oh, Junior, help!"

"What did you decide?"

"I think they were deciding to put up softball teams, the President and Secret Service and all that against some reporters. Only Hendricks Plantation doesn't have a softball field, of course. Who has? And Jake was saying, what would happen if the President of the United States got beaned by the Associated Press?"

"Really, Mister Neale," Junior said.

"Right," Neale said. "Mrs. March. . . ."

"At least the Vice-President plays golf," she said.

"At what time did you wake up, Mrs. March?"

87

"I'm not sure. Seven-fifteen? Seven-twenty? I heard the door to the suite close."

"That was me, Mister Neale," Junior said. "I went down to the lobby to get the newspapers."

"Walter had left his bed. It's always been a thing with him to be up a little earlier than I. A masculine thing. I heard him moving around the bathroom. I lay in bed a little while, a few minutes, really, waiting for him to be done."

"The bathroom door was closed?"

"Yes. In a moment I heard the television here in the living room go on, softly—one of those morning news and features network shows Walter always hated so much—so I got up and went into the bathroom."

"Excuse me. How did your husband get from the bathroom to the living room without coming back through your bedroom?"

"He went through Junior's bedroom, of course. He didn't want to disturb me."

"Mrs. March, are you saying that, in fact, you did not see your husband at all yesterday morning?"

"Oh, Captain Neale."

"I'm sorry. I mean, alive?"

"No. I didn't."

"Then how do you know it was he in the bathroom yesterday morning?"

"Captain, we've been married fifty years. You get used to the different sounds of your family. You know them, even in a hotel suite."

"Okay. You were in the bathroom. The television was playing softly in the living room. . . ."

"I heard the door to the suite close again, so I thought Walter had gone down for coffee."

"Had the television gone off?"

"No."

"So, actually, someone could have come into the suite at that point."

"No. At first, I thought Junior might have come back, but he couldn't have."

"Why not?"

"I didn't hear them talking."

"Would they have been talking? Necessarily?"

"Of course. About the headlines. The newspapers. The bulletins on the television. My husband and son are newspapermen, Captain Neale. Every day there are new developments. . . ."

"Yes. Of course."

"After getting the newspapers," Junior said, "I went into the coffee shop and had breakfast."

"So, Mrs. March, you think you heard the suite door close again, but your husband hadn't left the suite, and you think no one entered the suite because you didn't hear talking?"

"I guess that's right. I could be mistaken, of course. I'm trying to reconstruct."

"Pardon, but where were you physically in the bathroom when you heard the door close the second time?"

"I was getting into the tub. I don't shower in the morning. I discovered years ago that if I take a shower in the morning, I can never get my hair organized again, for the whole day."

"Yes. You had already run the tub?"

"Yes. While I was brushing my teeth. And all that."

"So there must have been a period of time, while the tub was running, that you couldn't have heard anything from the living room—not the front door, not the television, not talking?"

"I suppose not."

"So the second time you heard the door close, when you were getting into the tub, you actually could have been hearing someone leave the suite."

"Oh, my. That's right. Of course."

"It would explain your son's not having returned, your husband's not having left, and your not hearing talking."

"How clever you are."

"Then, what? You were sitting in the tub. . . ."

"I'm not sure. I think I heard the door open again. I believe I did. Because, later, when I went into the living room, when I . . . I . . . the door to the corridor was open."

"All right, Mother."

"I'm sorry, Captain Neale. This is difficult."

"Would you like to take a break? Get some coffee? Something?"

"Would you like an eye-opener, Captain Neale?"

"An eye-opener?"

"I'm making myself a Bloody Mary," Junior said.

"Oh, no, Junior," Lydia March said.

"A little early, for me," Neale said.

"Let's get it over with," Lydia said. "I heard Walter coughing. He never coughs. Not even in the morning. He's never smoked. . . . Then I heard him choking. It got worse. I called out, 'Walter! Are you all right? Walter!' "

"Take your time, Mrs. March."

"Then the choking stopped, and I thought he was all right. The telephone began ringing. Walter always picked up the phone on the first ring. It rang twice, it rang three times. I became very alarmed. I screamed, 'Walter!' I got out of the tub as fast as I could, grabbed a towel, opened the door to the bedroom. . . ."

"Which bedroom?"

"Ours. Walter's and mine. . . . Walter was sort of on the bed, the foot of the bed, his knees sort of on the floor, as if he hadn't quite made it to the bed . . . he had come from the living room . . . the bedroom door

90

was open . . . the scissors . . . I couldn't do a thing . . . he slipped sideways off the bed . . . Walter's a big man . . . I couldn't have caught him even if I had been able to move! He rolled as he slipped. He fell on his back . . . the scissors . . . face so white . . . Captain Neale, a big blood bubble came up between his lips. . . ."

"Mister March, why don't you give your mother some of that?"

"Come on, Mother."

"No, no. I'll be all right. Just give me a moment."

"Just a sip."

"No."

"We can postpone the rest of this, if you like, Mrs. March."

"I don't even remember going through the living room. I went through the open door to the corridor. I was just thinking, Helena, Helena, Jake . . . I knew they were in 7 . . . we had met for drinks there the night before . . . there was the back of a man . . . there was a man in the corridor walking away, lighting a cigar as he walked . . . I didn't know who he was, from behind . . . I ran toward him . . . then I realized who he was . . . I ran to Helena's door and began banging on it with my fist . . . Helena finally opened the door. She was in her bathrobe. Jake wasn't there. . . ."

"Mrs. March, did you go back into that suite?"

"My mother has not been back in that suite since."

"I was on Helena's bed. They left me alone. For a long time. I could hear people talking loudly, everywhere. Eleanor Earles came in. I asked her to find Junior. . . ."

"Did you know, at that point, your husband was dead?"

"I don't know what I knew. I knew he had landed on the scissors. I asked for someone to get Junior."

"And, Mister March?"

"I was in the coffee shop. I heard myself being paged in the lobby. Eleanor Earles was on a house phone. I came right up."

"What did Ms. Earles say to you, Mister March?"

"She said something had happened. My mother wanted me. She was in the Williams' suite—Number 7."

"She said, 'Something has happened'?"

"She said, 'Something has happened. Come up right away. This is Eleanor Earles. Your mother's in Jake Williams' suite—Number 7.' "

"What did all that mean to you?"

"I couldn't imagine why Eleanor Earles was calling me about anything. In the elevator I was thinking, maybe there had been an accident. I don't know what I was thinking."

"Mrs. March, are you all right?"

"Yes."

"Mrs. March. Who was the man in the corridor?"

"Perlman. Oscar Perlman."

"The humorist?"

"If you say so."

"Why didn't you speak to him?"

"Oh."

"I'm sorry? You said you ran toward him, and then you didn't speak to him."

She said, "Oscar Perlman has been very unkind to my husband. For years and years. Very unfair."

"Mother . . . realize what you're saying."

"I'm sorry, Mrs. March. You'll have to explain that."

"Well, years ago, Oscar used to work on one of the March family newspapers, and he thought he could write a humor column. He always was lazy. I've never thought him funny. Anyway, Walter encouraged him. He really developed the column for Oscar. Then, well, as soon as the column was established in one March

newspaper, Oscar went off and sold it—and himself—
to this syndicate. . . . Very unfair. Walter was terribly
hurt. Even last year, when Walter was nominated for
the presidency of the Alliance, Oscar was saying bad
things about him. Or, so we heard."

"What sort of bad things?"

"Oh, foolish things. Like he tried to pass a bylaw
saying only journalists could vote in the Alliance election, no private detectives."

" 'Private detectives'? What was that supposed to
mean?"

"Oh, who knows? Oscar Perlman's a fool."

"Mister March, do you know what 'no private detectives' means?"

"It doesn't mean anything," Walter March said.
"Oscar Perlman has a coterie of followers—mostly
Washington reporters—poker players all—and he keeps
them entertained with these sophomoric gags. I don't
know. March Newspapers is pretty well-known for its
investigative reporting. Maybe he was trying to make
some gag on that. I really don't know what it means.
No one did."

"Utter hateful foolishness," Lydia March said.

"Mrs. March, your husband was a powerful man.
He had been all his life. . . ."

"I know what you're about to ask, Captain Neale.
I've been lying awake, thinking about it myself. Walter
was a powerful man. Sometimes powerful men make
enemies. Not Walter. He was loved and respected.
Why, look, he was elected President of the American
Journalism Alliance. That's quite a tribute to a man—
from his colleagues, people he had worked with all his
life—now that Walter was, well, about to retire."

"Speaking of that, I'm a little uncertain. Who takes
over, who runs March Newspapers, now that your
husband. . . ."

"Why, Junior, of course. Junior's president of the company. Walter was chairman."

"I see."

"And Walter was retiring as soon as he had served out his term, here at the Alliance."

"I see."

"No one in this world, Captain, had reason to murder my husband. Why, you can see for yourself. In this morning's newspapers. Even on the television. Hy Litwack's nice eulogy last night. The reporters are terribly upset by this. Every one of them, Captain Neale, loved my husband."

Fourteen

11:00 A.M.

GOD IS IN MY TYPEWRITER, I KNOW IT
Address by Wharton Kruse
Conservatory

BULLDOGGING THE MAJOR MEDIA—OR BIRDDOGGING?
Weekly Newspapers Group Discussion
Bobby-Joe Hendricks Cocktail Lounge

"Mister Fletcher?"

Fletch squinted up from the poolside long chair at the young man in tennis whites, HENDRICKS PLANTATION written on his shirt.

"Yeah?"

"You phoned for a court at eleven o'clock?"

"I did?"

"I. M. Fletcher?"

"One of us is."

"We have you down for a tennis court at eleven o'clock."

"Thanks."

"Will you be needing equipment, sir?"

"I guess so. Also a partner. Playing tennis alone takes too much running back and forth."

"You mean, you want the pro?"

"I guess not. Someone means to provide me with exercise."

"Stop at the pro shop a little before eleven. We'll fix you up with a racket and balls—whatever you need. Have whites?"

"Send them to my room, will you? Room Seventy-nine."

"Sure. Thirty waist?"

"Guess so. Just ask the bellman to leave them inside the room. I have sneakers."

"Okay."

"Thanks," Fletch said.

A chair scraped next to him.

Fletch turned his head and squinted again.

"You're Fisher, aren't you?"

Stuart Poynton was sitting beside him, in expensive leisure clothes, green shirt, maroon slacks, yellow loafers—as pleasant to look at as lettuce, tomato soup, and a lemon.

"Fletcher," Fletch said.

"That's right. Fletcher. Someone told me about you."

"Someone tells you about everyone."

To be polite, one could refer to Stuart Poynton as a syndicated political columnist.

No one was ever polite about Stuart Poynton.

His columns demonstrated very little interest in politics—just politicians, and other power people.

His typical column had four to six hot, tawdry, indicative items (years ago, Senator So-and-so and his family had vacationed at a hunting lodge owned by a corporation his subcommittee is now regulating; Judge So-and-so was seen leaving a party in Georgetown at three in the morning; Congressman So-and-so fudged his fact-finding junket to Iran so he could visit his son in Zurich)—some of which were accurate enough to attract suits.

Always going for the jugular, in his desire to reform

others, over the years he had accomplished little—except to harden everyone's jugular.

"You know who I am?" he asked. "Poynton. Stuart Poynton."

"Oh," Fletch responded to this forced humility. "Nice to meetcha."

"Well, I was thinking this." Stuart Poynton was staring at his hands clasped between his knees, in thinking this. "Little hard for me to operate around here. Too much meeting and greeting going on. Well, point is, everyone here knows who I am, and everyone is sort of, you know, watching me." He looked sideways at Fletch. "Got me?"

"Gotcha."

"Makes it hard for me to operate, you know, carry on my own investigation. Find out anything. And this Walch March thing is a hell of a story."

"You mean Walter March?"

"I said Walter March. Point is, I can ask questions and so forth, but these idiotic conventioneers—well, you know, they seem to get a great kick out of giving Stuart Poynton a bum steer. Some of them have tried all ready. Jeez, you can't believe some of the crazy things they've told me around here—and with a straight face!"

Fletch said, "Gotcha."

"I can't blame 'em, of course. It's a convention after all. Fun and games are part of it."

Fletch had raised his chairback a few notches.

"Point is, I am Stuart Poynton." Again the sideways look. "Got me?"

"You got it right."

"And I am here."

"Gotcha."

"And the whole world knows that I'm here."

"Right."

"And here—here, at Kendricks Plantation—there's an important story."

"Hendricks Plantation."

"What?"

"Hendricks. *H,* as in waffle."

"I feel I ought to come up with something on the Walch March murder."

"Walter."

"You know, as a decent, self-respecting journalist. Some insight. Something indicative. You know, some little item or items that will mean something, prove to be right through the apprehension, trial, and conviction of the murderer."

"I don't see how you can do that without solving the crime."

"Well, that would help."

"Solving the Walter March murder would make a good item for your column," Fletch said mildly. "Might be worth a 'graf or two."

"Point is," Poynton said, "everyone knows I'm here. Everyone knows there's a big story here. But I'm so well-known here, if you get me, my hands are tied."

"Gotcha."

"Jack Williams tells me you're a hell of an investigative reporter."

"You mean Jake Williams?"

"That's what I said."

"Good old Howard."

"Yeah. Well, I asked him last night who he thought could help me out. You know, shag a few facts for me. You're unemployed?"

"Presently unencumbered by earned income."

"You have no outlet?"

"Only the kind you can flush."

"I mean, if you had a story, it would probably be difficult for you to get it published?"

"There's no front page being held for me."

"I thought not. Maybe we can work something out. What I'm thinking is this." Poynton again went into his staring-at-hands-clasped-between-his-knees propositional pose. "You be my eyes and ears. You know— do legwork. Circulate. Talk to them. Listen to them. If you do any keyhole stuff, I don't want to know about it. Just the facts—all I want. See what you can dig up. Report to me."

Fletch let the next question hang silent in the air.

Poynton sat back in his chair. " 'Pending on what you come up with, of course—when I get back to New York—well, maybe I could use another legman."

" 'Maybe'?"

"The three I have are pretty well-known. Which is why I can't bring them in here. Everyone in the business knows who they are. In fact, they've about served their purpose."

"Hell of an offer," Fletch said.

Poynton glanced at him nervously.

"Legman for Walter Poynton. Wow!"

"Stuart," said Stuart Poynton.

Fletch looked at him, puzzled.

" 'Course, I'd pick up your expenses here at the convention, too," Poynton said, " 'cause you'd be working for me." Poynton turned full-face to Fletch. "What do you say. Will you do it?"

"You bet."

"You will?"

"Sure."

"Shake on it." Poynton held out his hand, and they shook. "Now," he said, reclasping his hands, "what have you got so far?"

"Not much," Fletch said. "I haven't really been working."

"Come on," Poynton said. "Reporter's instincts. . . ."

"Just arrived yesterday. . . ."

"Must have heard a few things. . . ."

"Well . . . of course."

"Like what?"

"Well, I heard something funny about the desk clerk."

"The desk clerk here at the hotel?"

"Yeah. Seems Walter March got very angry when he arrived. Desk clerk made some fresh crack at Mrs. March. March took his name and said he was going to report him to the manager in the morning. . . . Someone said the clerk's pretty heavily in debt. You know—the horses."

"That would tie in with the scissors," Poynton said.

"What scissors?"

"The scissors," Poynton said. "The scissors found in Walch March's back. They came from the reception desk in the lobby."

"Wow!" said Fletch.

"Also the timing of the murder."

"What do you mean?"

"The clerk would have to nail March before he left his room in the morning. Before the hotel manager arrived at work. Before March had a chance to report the clerk to the manager."

"Hey," Fletch said. "That's right!"

"Another thing," Poynton said. "There's been the question of how anyone got into the suite to murder March in the first place."

Fletch said, "I don't get you."

"The desk clerk!" Poynton said. "He'd have the key."

"Wow," Fletch said. "Right!"

Again the nervous glance from Poynton.

"Sounds worth investigating," he said. "See what you can dig up."

"Yes, sir."

Three youngsters were throwing something into the pool and then diving after it.

"I heard something else," Poynton said.

"Oh? What?"

"Ronny Wisham."

Fletch said, "You mean Rolly Wisham?"

"That's what I said."

"Must be the noise from the pool."

"Seems Walch March had started an editorial campaign to get this Wisham character fired from the network, and ordered March newspapers coast-to-coast to follow up."

"Really? Why would he do that?"

"Apparently this Wisham is one of these bleeding-heart reporters. An advocate journalist."

"Yeah."

Rolly Wisham did features for one of the networks, and they were usually on Society's downside—prisoners, mental patients, migrant workers, welfare mothers. He always ended his reports saying, "This is Rolly Wisham, with love."

"Son of a bitch," said Fletch.

"March thought he was unprofessional. As President of the A.J.A. he wanted Ronny Wisham drummed out of journalism."

"That would be a motive for murder, all right," Fletch said. "Walter March could have succeeded in a campaign like that—to get rid of someone."

"Jack Williams confirmed last night that these articles were going to run. Then there'd be an incessant campaign against this Ronny Wisham character."

"And these articles are not going to run now?"

"No. Jack Williams feels beatin' up on somebody like Ronny Wisham would result in a sort of bad image for Walch March."

"I see," said Fletch. "Very clear."

Freddie Arbuthnot appeared around the hedge.

She was wearing tennis whites and carrying a racket.

"Williams said he was sure the other managing editors in the chain would feel the same way."

"Sure," said Fletch.

Poynton saw Freddie approaching them, and stood up.

"See what you can dig up," he said.

"Thanks, Mister Poynton."

Fletch got out of the long chair and introduced Fredericka Arbuthnot and Stuart Poynton by saying, "Ms. Blake, I'd like you to meet Mister Gesner."

As they shook hands, Poynton gave Fletch a glance of gratitude and Freddie gave him her usual *You're weird* look.

After Poynton ambled away, Freddie said, "You get along well with everybody."

"Sure," Fletch said. "I'm very amiable."

"That was Stuart Poynton," she said.

"Are you sure?"

"Why did you introduce him as whatever?"

"Are you Ms. Blake?"

"I am not Ms. Blake."

"Are you Freddie Arbuthnot?"

"I am Freddie Arbuthnot."

"Are you sure?"

"I've looked it up."

"You have nice knees. Very clean. Hoo, boy!"

She blushed, slightly, beneath her tan.

"You've been listening through my bathroom wall."

"Whatever do you mean?"

"That was a little song I was taught. As a child." She was blushing more. "The 'Wash Me Up' song."

"Oh!" Fletch said. "There is a difference between boys and girls! I was taught the wash-me-down song!"

She put her fist between his ribs and pushed.

"There's a difference between people and horses," she said. "People and weirdos."

"Playing tennis?" he asked.

"Thought I might."

"You have a partner, of course."

"Actually, I don't."

"Odd," said Fletch. "There seems to be a court reserved in my name. Eleven o'clock."

"And no partner?"

"None I know of."

"That is odd," she said. "One ought to have a partner, to play tennis."

"Indeed."

"Makes the game nicer."

"I suspect so."

"Would you please go get dressed?"

"Why are people always saying that to me?"

"I suspect people aren't always saying that to you."

"Oh, well," said Fletch.

"Ms. Blake is waiting for you," Freddie Arbuthnot said softly. "Patiently."

Fifteen

12:00 Cocktails
   Bobby-Joe Hendricks Lounge

From TAPE
Station 17
Room 102 (Crystal Faoni)
   "Hi, Bob? Is this Robert McConnell?

   "This is Crystal Faoni . . . Crystal Faoni. We sat at the same table last night. I was the big one in the flower-print tent. . . . Yeah, isn't she gorgeous? That's Fredericka Arbuthnot. I'm the other one. The one twice the size people spend half the time looking at. . . .

   "Say, I really dig you, Bob. I think you're great. I read your stuff all the time. . . .

   "Yeah, I read your piece this morning. On the murder of Walter March. You mentioned Fletcher, uh? Fletcher. We used to work together. On a newspaper in Chicago. You really put it to him, didn't you . . . what was it you wrote? Something about Fletch's already having figured prominently in two murder cases but never indicted . . . and he used to work for Walter March . . . ?

   "Let me tell you something about Fletch. . . .

   "Useful information? Why, sure, honey. . . .

   "Just a funny story, really. . . .

   "See, there was this guy in Chicago Fletch didn't like much, a real badass named Upsie . . . a pimp running

104

a whole string of girls in Chicago, real young kids, fourteen, fifteen, sixteen-year-olds, pickin' 'em up at the bus station the minute they hit town, pilling them up, then shooting them up, putting them straight on the street sometimes the same damn' night they hit town.

"As soon as the kids got to the point where they couldn't stand up anymore, couldn't even attract fleas—which was usually a few months, at most—like as not they'd be found overdosed in some alley or run over by a car. You know?

"A big, nasty business Upsie was running. This fast turnover in girls meant there was very little live evidence against him, ever. What's more, he could pay off heavy, in all directions, up and down the fuzz ladder. . . .

"This was a very slippery badass.

"Fletch wanted the story. He wanted the details. He wanted the hard evidence.

" 'Course he got no cooperation from the police.

"And the newspaper wasn't cooperating, either. The editors, they said, you know, what's one pimp? It isn't worth the space to run the story. Typical.

"And Fletch wasn't doing this precisely right, either.

"Every time he talked a girl into his confidence and began getting stuff he could use as evidence, he'd realize what he was doing, what he was asking them to do, in turning state's evidence—allow themselves to be dragged through the newspapers and television and courts for months, if not years.

"Upsie had already badly damaged their lives in one way.

"Fletch saw himself badly damaging their lives in another way.

"These kids were so young, Bob. . . .

"Anyway, as soon as Fletch got the story from each girl, instead of using it, he found himself getting her to a social service agency, a hospital, or getting up the

105

scratch to bus her home—whatever he thought would work.

"He did this six, eight times maybe.

"Well, Upsie got upset. He was pretty sure, I guess, Fletch wasn't going to be able to print anything on him, ever, what with no police support, no newspaper support, and while Fletch kept sending his best sources of evidence home on a bus . . . but nevertheless, Fletch was hurting Upsie's business by continually taking these girls away from Upsie before they were ready to be wiped.

"Get the point?

"So Upsie sends a couple of goons out, and they find Fletch, drag him out of his car—a real honey, a dark green Fiat convertible, I loved it—and while they hold him at a distance, arms behind his back, they put a fuse in the gas tank and light it and the car blows all over the block.

"The goons say, 'Upsie's upset. Next time the fuse goes up your ass, and it won't be just gas at the other end.'

"So next night—it was a Saturday night—Fletch finds Upsie getting out of his pimpmobile and goes up to him as smooth as cream cheese, hand out to shake, and says, 'Upsie, I apologize. Let me buy you a drink.' Just like that. Upsie's wary at first, but figures, hell, Fletch is aced, he's aced other people easily enough, maybe it might be nice to have someone on the newspaper he has in his pocket, whatever. . . .

"Fletch takes him into the nearest dive, buys Upsie a drink, tries to explain he was just doing his job, but, what the hell, what did the newspaper care, he could end up dead on the sidewalk for all the newspaper cared.

"He had brought a little pill with him—something one of Upsie's own girls had given him—and when

Upsie was nice and relaxed and beginning to tell Fletch about his having been a nine-year-old newspaper boy on the South Side, Fletch slips the pill into Upsie's gin.

"In a very few minutes, Upsie's swaying, doesn't know what the hell he's doing, begins to pass out, and Fletch, still as smooth as canned apple sauce, walks him out and puts Upsie in the passenger's seat of the pimpmobile at the curb. See?

"He drives Upsie to this heavy, ornate Episcopal church Fletch knows about—knows how to get into that hour of Saturday night—and helps him into the church and sits him on the floor, where Upsie passes out.

"On the floor, Fletch strips Upsie of all his pimp finery.

"Then he places him spread-eagled on his back in the center aisle, bareass, badass naked, and ties his wrists and ankles to the last few pews—did I say spread-eagled?—in the dark.

"Then he takes a thin wire and ties it up around Upsie's balls—around his penis, you know?—and runs that straight and fairly taut to the huge brass doorknob of the heavy front door of the church. There's a purple velvet drape around the door, and the door is solid oak.

"He ties the wire nice and tight to the doorknob.

"Then Fletch goes up to the altar and drags the bishop's chair over so he can sit in it and see Upsie 'way down the center aisle, but Upsie can't see him.

"By and by, Upsie wakes up and groans, obviously not feeling too well, and tries to roll over and finds he's tied to something, all four points, and wakes up more, and tugs at the ropes, and then raises his head to look down at himself and finds he's tied at his fifth point, too.

"He can't see too well in the dark, probably well enough to see that he's in a church, and he remains reasonably relaxed, still groggy from the liquor and the drug, probably curious about what's happening to him, tied spread-eagled and naked, lying on a church floor.

"It's dawn, and light comes into the church, all red and blue and yellow in streaks through the big stained-glass windows, and the wire begins to pick up the light and gleam, and Upsie has his head up all the time, now, as much as his neck muscles can stand it, trying to see where the wire leads.

"In a while there's enough light in the church to start getting into the draped, recessed doorway, and shortly the big, brass doorknob begins to gleam—even Fletch can see it from the altar—and it's clear even from where he's sitting that the wire leads straight from Upsie's balls to the doorknob of these doors which must weigh a ton.

"Upsie sees it too, of course, and begins to figure it out, begins tugging at his ropes, flexing one arm, and then the other, pulling each leg up against the ropes.

"He realizes there's no way he's going to get free, unless someone helps him.

"But he doesn't get the real point of what's happening to him—or what's going to happen to him—until the church bells begin to ring, all over Chicago. It's then he begins shouting, 'Oh, no! Oh, God! Oh, no!'

"He remembers it's Sunday morning and at some point, sooner or later, those heavy oak doors are going to be swung open by hundreds of joyous Christians, en masse, you might say, strong in their faith.

"It's then that Upsie's body fluids begin leaving him. In sheer terror, he pisses almost to the church door, like a skunk shooting at something he knows is going to destroy him. He's lying in his own shit, just tons of it, pouring out of him.

"He's sweating buckets and shaking and pulling at his ropes.

"He knows that when those heavy oak doors are swung open, he's had it.

"Did I say he was yelling? He's yelling and screaming, first the words, 'Help me! Help me, someone!' in this cavernous church with solid stone walls, and then he's yelling every obscenity in the book, in furious anger, tugging at the ropes so hard his wrists and ankles burn through, bleeding, and then he begins to blubber, 'I don't deserve this, I don't deserve this,' and, crying. He thinks about this awhile, and then begins twisting his head toward the altar, yelling, 'Oh, God, I'm sorry! I'm sorry!'

"Fletch picked the right church.

"This particular church didn't have Sunday service until eleven in the morning.

"But a lot of other churches in town had services before then.

"And every time one of the other churches' bells begins to ring, Upsie pulls harder on his ropes, the ropes tying him. He wears the ropes right down to his wrist and ankle bones.

"He even begins biting his left arm, through the muscle, thinking he would chew his arm off, I guess, until he realizes that would do no good: If he chewed off one arm, he still wouldn't be able to untie the rest of himself. See?

"More and more church bells ring around town, calling their congregations to service, and Upsie is screaming more and more incomprehensively, very hoarse by now, convulsively tugging at his ropes, ever one more time, hoping something would give way, blood and shit all over himself, eyes bulging from his head.

"At ten-thirty—after hours of this—the church bells of that church begin to go off, and Upsie becomes even more frantic. He knows it's only a few minutes now, at most, before that heavy oak door is swung open.

"He's thrashing around the floor, as much as the ropes will let him, twisting and splashing in his own blood and shit.

"Even Fletch couldn't hear him yelling over the sound of the church bells. He could just see his mouth open, jaws straining, tongue extended. Upsie's eyes are rolling in his head, in terror.

"Then the big brass doorknob begins to turn, slowly, slowly.

"Upsie stiffens his body, tries to reach his hands down to his balls—of course they don't reach—actually tries to pull away from the door. . . .

"Oh, by the way, will I see you at lunch, Bob? The menu said something about chicken Divan or salad of your choice. Knowing me, I expect I'll have both. . . .

"What do you mean, 'What happened'? I told you it's a funny story. Fletch is a funny man. . . .

"You can't figure out what happened?

"Jeez, Bob, you're no better than Upsie.

"The church doors swung inward, Bob. Upsie couldn't see that, because of the drapes. . . .

"Fletcher? Oh, he left through the sacristy door.

"Gee, Bob, I thought you knew Fletcher. . . ."

Sixteen

From TAPE
Station 22
Room 42 (Leona Hatch)

"Ready for lunch?"

"Just putting on my hat."

"Why do you need a hat? We're not leaving the building."

"If your hair were as thin as mine, Nettie. . . ."

"I'd never leave the house," Nettie Horn said. "You feel you must have a trademark, Leona. As if anybody cared."

"I like wearing a hat."

"With your vanity, I just don't understand how you let yourself get so drunk."

"What do you mean?"

"You didn't make it to dinner last night, Leona."

"You did?"

"I did."

"And what happened to you after dinner, Nettie?"

"I'm not perfectly sure. I seem to remember singing around a piano. . . ."

"Nettie, I put myself to bed in a proper manner last night. I even folded my clothes and removed my corset and got under the covers. In fact, I totally unraveled my corset. That took great concentration and deliberation—although why I felt I had to do it, I don't know.

111

Had a dickens of a time putting it all together again this morning. Where did you sleep last night?"

"I woke up in a chair in my room."

"Fully dressed?"

"Well. . . ."

"I know you, Nettie. Somebody just dumped you there. Probably a bellman. Well, I was in my bed with my corset off. Now, don't give me any more of your nonsense about *my* being drunk in public. . . ."

Fletch switched off the marvelous machine to answer his phone.

"Fletcher, old buddy, old friend!"

"Don?"

"Yes, sir, I'm here."

"If this is Don Gibbs, I thought we established when I called you from Washington that we are not buddies, not friends, but, at the most, useless acquaintances."

"How can you say that? Come on. Didn't we learn the Northwestern fight song together?"

"I never learned beyond the first verse."

"What could be verse?" Don Gibbs said.

"Learning the second verse. Golly, Don, you sound full of bonhomie."

"Does that taste anything like Wild Turkey bourbon?"

"You government guys drink good stuff."

"Seldom do I personally get the opportunity to squeeze the taxpayer's wallet. How goes the convention?"

"If I ask where you are will I get an answer?"

"Try it and see."

"Where are you, Don?"

"Here."

"Terrific. Can you be a little more precise as to where 'here' is, geographically, at the moment?"

112

"Hendricks Plantation. Hendricks, Virginia. U. S. of A."

"Here?"

"You've got it."

"What are you doing here?"

"Thought we'd come along to see how you're doing."

" 'We'?"

"Bob is with me."

"Who's Bob?"

"Bob Englehardt, my honored and beloved department head."

"What are you doing here?"

"This Walter March murder, Fletch. It sort of worries us."

"Why should it? What's the C.I.A. got to do with it? The murder of a private citizen within the United States is a purely domestic matter."

"March Newspapers has foreign bureaus, hasn't it?"

"Boy, you guys have elastic minds."

"By the way, how much poop have you got on the murder?"

"I've got it solved."

"Really?"

"Yeah."

"Out with it."

"No."

"Wait a minute, Fletch. Bob wants to speak to you. I'll come back on the line."

"Mister Fletcher?" Robert Englehardt was trying to lighten his ponderous tone. "May I call you Fletch?"

"I don't know why you call me at all."

"Well, to answer that question, we need you to cover for us. Don has been calling your room since we arrived, so you wouldn't express surprise at seeing us at the various functions here at the hotel and blurt out our actual employer."

"I was playing tennis with What's-her-name."

"Who? What is her name?"

"Exactly."

"Fletch, we're here as observers from the Canadian press."

"Anyone in Canada know that?"

"No. Our official story is that we're thinking of setting up a similar convention, next year, in Ontario. Naturally, we expect you to allow no one here, now or ever, to know whom we actually represent."

"Why in hell should I cover for you guys?"

"For all of the above reasons."

"Again?"

"Failure to file federal tax returns, evasion of federal taxes, deporting United States currency illegally. . . ."

"I've always heard it's more difficult to keep a fortune than to make one."

"Then we have your complete cooperation?"

"How could you think otherwise?"

Robert Englehardt said, "Good. Here's Don."

After a pause in which the clink of an ice cube against a glass was audible, Don Gibbs said, "Fletch?"

"Gee, Don. Your superior didn't say he was looking forward to meeting me."

"Actually, Fletch," Don said, "he's not."

"Gee, Don."

"How's the taping going? Got much dirt yet?"

"It's a marvelous machine. Very sensitive."

"What do you have so far? Anything good?"

"Mostly toilets flushing, showers running, typewriters clacking, and a lot of journalists talking to themselves in their rooms. I never realized journalists are such lonely people."

"That all?"

"No, I also have a complete tape of the *New World* Symphony from somebody's radio."

114

"You must have more than that."

"People snoring, coughing, sneezing. . . ."

"Okay, Fletch. Expect we'll see you around."

"Never saw you before in my life. By the way, Don, what room are you in?"

"Suite 3. They had to give us the suite in which Walter March was murdered. They didn't have any other place to put us."

"Really living it up, uh?"

"The rule book says we can take a suite if nothing else is available."

"I'm glad I'm not a taxpayer," Fletch said. "Bye."

Fletch switched his marvelous machine to Station 5—Suite 3.

". . . Turkey in school," Don Gibbs was saying. "Always out doing his own thing."

"More?" Robert Englehardt said.

"No one could ever figure out what it was. Gone night after night. Never came to the parties. Used to make jokes about Fletch. They always began with, 'Where's Fletch?' and then someone would make up something ridiculous, like, 'Sniffing the bicycle seats outside the girls' dorms. . . .' "

"Come on. Finish your drink. Let's go to lunch."

"Hey, Bob. We're supposed to be journalists, aren't we? Journalists live it up. I saw a movie once. . . ."

Seventeen

1:00 P.M. Lunch
Main Dining Room

Arriving late at lunch, Fletch put his hand out to Robert McConnell, who was already looking warily at him from his place at the round table, and said, "Bob, I apologize. Let me buy you a drink."

Robert McConnell's jaw dropped, his eyes bugged out, and he turned white.

Robert McConnell bolted from the table, and, from the room.

Crystal Faoni was staring at Fletch.

Fletch said to her, "What's the matter with him? Just trying to apologize for accusing him of murder. . . ."

Freddie Arbuthnot looked clean and fresh after their tennis. Clearly she had sung her "Hoo, boy" song again.

Lewis Graham had taken one of the empty seats at the table, and Fletch shook hands with him, saying, "Slumming, eh?"

The man shook hands as would an eel—if eels were familiar with human social graces.

Lewis Graham was a television network's answer to the newspaper editorial.

A gray man with a long face and narrow chin, who apparently confused looking distinguished and intellectual with looking sad and tired, every night for ninety polysyllabic seconds he machine-gunned his audience with informed, intellectual opinion on some event or situation of the day or the week, permitting the people of America to understand there were facts they didn't have yet and probably wouldn't be able to comprehend if they did have them, without his experience, and understandings they could never have, without his incisive intelligence.

Trouble was, his colleagues read the *New York Times,* the *Washington Post,* the *Atlanta Constitution,* the *Los Angeles Times, Time, Newsweek, Foreign Affairs,* and the Old Testament as well as he and could identify the sources of his facts, insights, and understandings, precisely, night after night.

Other journalists referred to Lewis Graham as "the *Reader's Digest* of the air."

It was questioned whether behind his grayness he had any personality he had not lifted from newsprint.

Lewis Graham said, "I didn't know where to sit. I expect lunch is the same at all the tables."

Crystal Faoni was still staring at Fletch after he sat down.

Freddie said, "A fairly even match, if I may say so. Six-four you; six-four me; seven-five us."

"Me," said Fletch.

"It was just your chauvinist pride."

"Me," said Fletch. "Me."

"Not a clear victory. Your arms and legs are longer than mine."

"The thing about tennis," Lewis Graham said, "is that someone has to win, and someone has to lose."

Crystal turned her stare at Lewis Graham.

They all stared at Lewis Graham.

"Tennis always provides a clear victory," Lewis Graham said.

Fletch asked, "Did you read that somewhere?"

Crystal said to Fletch, "I ordered you both the chicken Divan and the chef's salad."

"Thank you for thinking of me," Fletch said. "I don't want both."

"You want one of them?"

"Yes. I want one of them."

"Then I'll have the other one. Well, why should I embarrass myself by ordering two meals for myself—when I can embarrass you instead? You need a little embarrassing."

"Why should you be embarrassed?"

"Oh, come off it, Fletch," Crystal Faoni said. "Have you ever made love to a really fat girl?"

Graham shifted his elbows uncomfortably on the table.

"I'll weigh the question," Fletch said.

"As fat as I am?"

Fletch said, "It's a heavy question."

Lewis Graham cleared his throat and said, "You appear to be giving light answers."

During the lunch (Fletch ate the salad; Crystal ate two Divans, which caused Lewis Graham to quip that all she needed more to entertain was a fireplace and a coffee table), the topic of Walter March's murder arose, and, after listening awhile to Graham's reporting what he had read in the morning newspapers, complete with two Old Testament references to the transitory nature of life, Crystal raised her large, beautiful head from the trough and said, "You know, I heard Walter March announce his retirement."

"I didn't know he had," said Graham.

"He did."

"So what?" Freddie asked. "He was over seventy."

"It was more than five years ago."

"Men look forward to their retirements with mixed feelings," said Graham. "On the one hand, they desire retirement in their weariness. On the other, they shirk from the loss of power, the vacuum, the . . . uh . . . retirement which is attendant upon uh . . . ," he said, ". . . retirement."

Crystal, Freddie, and Fletch stared at Lewis Graham again.

"Was it a public announcement?" Fletch asked.

"Oh, yes," Crystal answered. "A deliberate, official, public announcement. It was at the opening of the new newspaper plant in San Francisco. I was covering. There was a reception, you see, big names and gowns and things, so of course the darling editors sent a woman to write it all up. There were scads of those little hors d'oeuvres, you know, chicken livers wrapped in bacon, duck and goose pâtés, landing fields of herring in sour cream. . . ."

"Crystal," Fletch said.

"What?"

"Are you hungry?"

"No, thanks. I'm having lunch."

"Get on with the story, please."

"Anyway, Walter March was to make one of those wowee, whizbang, look at our new plant, look at us, what an accomplishment speeches, and he did. But he also took the occasion to announce his retirement. He said he was sixty-five and he had instituted and enforced the retirement age of sixty-five throughout the company and although he understood better how people felt reaching sixty-five, being forced to retire, when he felt in the prime of his life, years of experience behind him, years of energy ahead of him, wasted, blah, blah, he was no exception to his own rules, he was retiring himself."

"I guess, ultimately, he considered himself an exception to his own rules," Freddie said.

"He always did," said Lewis Graham.

"He even said he was having his boat brought around to San Diego and was looking forward to sailing the South Pacific with wife of umpty-ump years, Lydia. He painted quite a picture. Sailing off into the sunset, hand in hand with his childhood sweetheart, sitting on his poop or whatever it is yachts have."

"He owned a big catamaran, didn't he?" Freddie asked.

"A trimaran," said Lewis Graham. "Three hulls. I chartered it once."

"You did?" Fletch said.

"A few years ago. The *Lydia*. I used to consider Walter March sort of a friend."

"What happened?" Fletch said. "Boat spring a leak?"

Lewis Graham shrugged.

"I don't see anything unusual in this," Freddie Arbuthnot said. "Lots of people get cold feet when it comes time to retire."

Fletch said, "Did he say when he was going to retire, Crystal? I mean, did he give any definite time?"

"In six months. The new plant was opened in December, and I clearly remember his saying he and Lydia were westward-hoing in June."

"He was definite?"

"Definite. I reported it. We all did. It's in the files. 'WALTER MARCH ANNOUNCES RETIREMENT.' And he said the greatest joy of his life was that he was leaving March Newspapers in good hands."

"Whose?" Freddie asked.

Crystal said, "Guess."

"The little bastard," Lewis Graham said. "Junior."

"I saw him this morning," Crystal said. "In the elevator. Boy, does he look awful. Dead eyes staring out of a white face. You'd think he'd died, instead of his father."

"Understandable," said Fletch.

"Junior looked like he was going somewhere to lie down quietly in a coffin," Crystal said. "Everyone in the elevator was silent."

"So," Fletch said, "why didn't Walter March retire when he said he was going to? Is that the question?"

"Because," Lewis Graham said, "the bastard wanted to be President of the American Journalism Alliance. That's the simple reason. He wanted it badly. I can tell you how badly he wanted it."

Graham saw the three of them staring at him again, realized how forcefully he had spoken, and relaxed in his chair.

He said, "I'm just saying he wanted to cap his career with the presidency of the A.J.A. He spoke to me about it years ago. He was canvassing for support, eight, ten years ago."

"Did you offer him your support?" Fletch asked.

"Of course I did. Then. He had a few years to go before retirement, and I had a whole decade. Then."

The waiter was pouring the coffee.

"Two or three times," Lewis Graham continued, "he got his name placed in nomination. I never did. And he never won." Graham pushed the coffee cup away from him. "Until last year. Both our names were placed in nomination."

"I see," Fletch said.

"Well," Graham said, "I don't have the advantage Walter March had—I don't own my own network." Graham looked a little abashed. "I have to retire the first of this year. There's no way I can hang on."

Crystal said, "And the A.J.A. bylaws say our officers have to be working journalists."

"Right," Graham said with surprising bitterness. "Not retired journalists."

"Is that why you stopped considering Walter March

121

a friend?" asked Freddie. "Because you opposed each other in an election?"

"Oh, no," said Graham. "I'm an old man, now, with much experience. Especially political. There are very few things in the course of elections I haven't seen. I've witnessed some very dirty campaigns, in my time." Graham deferred to the younger people at the table. "I guess we all have. One just never expects to be the victim of such a campaign."

A bellman was having Fletch pointed out to him by the headwaiter.

Graham said, "I guess you all know Walter March kept a whole barnyard full of private detectives?"

Crystal, Freddie, Fletch said nothing.

Graham sat back in his chair.

"End of story," he said.

The bellman was standing next to Fletch's chair.

"Telephone, Mister Fletcher," he said. "Would you come with me?"

Fletch put down his napkin and rose from his seat.

"I wouldn't bother you, sir," the bellman said, "except they said it's the Pentagon calling."

Eighteen

"One moment, sir. Major Lettvin calling."

Fletch had been led to a wall phone down the corridor from the entrance to the dining room.

Leaving the dining room, he had seen (and ignored) Don Gibbs.

Through the plate glass window at the end of the corridor, a couple of meters away, he could see the midday sunlight shimmering on the car tops in the parking lot.

"How do," the Major said. "Do I have the honor of addressing Irwin Maurice Fletcher?"

The drawl was thicker than Mississippi mud.

"Right," said Fletch.

"Veteran of the United States Marine Corps?"

"Yes."

"Serial Number 1893983?"

"It was. I retired it. Anyone can use it now."

"Well, sir, some sharp-eyed old boy here in one of our clerical departments, reading about that murder in the newspaper, you know, what's his name? where you at?"

The drawl was so steeped in courtesy everything sounded like a question.

After a moment, Fletch said, "Walter March."

"Walter March. Say, you're right in the middle of things again, aren't ya?"

Fletch said, "Middle of lunch, actually."

"Anyway, this here sharp-eyed old boy—he's from Tennessee—I suspect he was pretty well-known around home for shooting off hens' teeth at a hundred meters— well, anyway, reading this story in the newspaper about Walter March's murder, he spotted your name?"

Again, it sounded like a question.

Fletch said, "Yes."

"Say, you aren't a suspect or anything in this murder, are ya?"

"No."

"What I mean to say is, you're not implicated in this here murder in any way, are ya?"

"I wasn't even here when it was committed. I was flying over the Atlantic. I was coming from Italy."

"Well, the way this story is written, it makes you wonder. Why do journalists do things like this? Ask me, take all the journalists in the world, put 'em in a pot, and all you've got is fishbait." Major Lettvin paused. "Oops. Sorry. You're a journalist, aren't ya? I forgot that for a moment. Sportswriters I don't mind so much."

"I'm not a sportswriter."

"Well, he recognized your name—how many Irwin Maurice Fletchers can there be?" (Fletch restrained himself from saying, "I don't know.") "And checked against our files here at the P-gon, and, sure enough, there you were. Serial Number 1893983. That you?"

"Major, do you have a point? This is long distance. You never can tell. A taxpayer might be listening in."

"That's right." The Major chuckled. "That's right."

There was a long silence.

"Major?"

"Point is, we've been lookin' for ya, high and low, these many years."

"Why?"

"Says here we owe you a Bronze Star. Did you know that?"

"I heard a rumor."

"Well, if you knew it, how come you've never arranged to get decorated?"

"I. . . ."

"Seems to me, if a fella wins a Bronze Star he ought to get it pinned to his chest. These things are important."

"Major, it's nice of you to call. . . ."

"No problem, no problem. Just doin' my duty. We got so many people here at the P-gon, everybody doin' each other's lazying, it's a sheer pleasure to have something to do—you know what I mean?—to separate breakfast from supper."

There was a man ambling across the parking lot, hands in the back pockets of his jeans.

"You going to be there a few days, Mister Fletcher?"

"Where?"

"Wherever you are. Hendricks Plantation, Hendricks, Virginia."

"Yes."

The man in the parking lot wore a blue jeans jacket.

"Well, I figure what I'll do is dig up a general somewhere—believe me, that's not difficult around the P-gon—we've got more generals in one coffee shop than Napoleon had in his whole army—we could decorate the Statue of Liberty with 'em, and you'd never see the paint peel—and move his ass down to Hendricks, Virginia. . . ."

"General? I mean, Major?"

The man in the parking lot also had tight, curly gray hair.

"I figure a presentation ceremony, in front of all those journalists—decorating one of their own, so to speak, with a Bronze Star. . . ."

The man who had accosted Mrs. Leary in the parking lot.

"Major? I've got to go."

"The Marine Corps could use some good press, these days, you know. . . ."

"Major. I've got to go. An emergency. My pants are on fire. Call me back."

Fletch hung up, turned around, and headed down the corridor at high speed.

He found a fire door with EXIT written over it, pushed through it, and ran down the stairs.

He entered the parking area slowly, trying not to make it too obvious he was looking for someone.

No one else was in the parking lot.

The man had been walking toward the back of the area.

Fletch went to the white rail fence and walked along it, looking down the slope to his right.

He caught a glimpse of the man crossing behind two stands of rhododendrons.

He sprung over the fence and ran down the slope.

When he ran through the opening in the rhododendrons, and stopped, abruptly, to look around, he saw the man standing under some apple trees, hands in back pockets, looking at him.

Slowly, Fletch began to walk toward him.

The man took his hands out of his pockets, turned, and ran, further down the slope, toward a large stand of pine. Behind the pine trees were the stables.

Fletch noticed he was wearing sneakers.

Fletch ran after him, and when he came to the pine trees, his shoes began to slip on the slope. To brake himself from falling, he grabbed at a scrub pine, got sap on his hands, and fell.

Looking around from the ground, Fletch could neither see nor hear the man.

Fletch picked himself up and walked through the pines to the stable area, trying to scrape the sap off his hands with his thumbnails.

In the midday sun, the stables had the quiet of a long lunch hour typical of a place where people work early and late. No one was there.

For a few minutes Fletch petted the horse he had ridden that morning, asking her if she had seen a man run by (and answering for her, "He went thet-away"), and then walked back to the hotel.

Nineteen

2:00 P.M.

VARIOUS USES OF COMPUTERS IN JOURNALISM
Address by Dr. Hiram Wong
Parlor

From TAPE
Station 1
Suite 12 (Mrs. Walter March and Walter March, Jr.)

"Bandy called from Los Angeles, Junior. Some question he can't deal with. And Masur called asking if he should put that basketball scandal on the wires from New York. . . ."

There was no answer.

"Are you having lunch?" Lydia asked her son.

No answer.

"Oh, for God's sake, Junior. Buck up! Your father's dead, and someone has to make the decisions for the newspapers. They can't run themselves. They never have."

Another silence.

"I'm ordering you lunch," she said. "You can't Bloody Mary yourself to death. . . ."

From TAPE
Station 9
Room 36 (Rolly Wisham)

"If you'll permit me a question first, Captain Neale. . . ."

"I don't know. Once you journalists start asking questions, you never stop. I've had enough opportunity to discover that."

"Very simply: Why are you questioning me?"

"We understand you might have had a motive to murder Walter March."

"Oh?"

Rolly Wisham's voice did not have great timbre, for a man nearly thirty, but there was a boy's aggressiveness in it, mixed with an odd kindliness.

Listening to the tape, sitting on his bed, picking at the sap on his hands, Fletch kept expecting Wisham to say, "This is Rolly Wisham, with love"—as if such meant anything to anybody, especially in journalism.

"What motive do you think I would have for murdering the old bastard?"

"I know about the editorial that ran in the March newspapers calling your television feature reporting— have I the term right?—let's see, it called it 'sloppy, sentimental, and stupendously unprofessional.' That's precise. I had the editorial looked up and read to me over the phone this noon."

"That's what it said."

"I also know that this editorial was just the beginning of a coast-to-coast campaign to put you in disgrace and get you fired from the network. Every March newspaper was to follow up with articles punching holes in your every statement, every report, day by day."

"I didn't know that, but I guessed it."

"Walter March had begun a smear campaign against you. Frankly, Mister Wisham, I didn't know such things happen nowadays."

"Call me Rolly."

"I think of that kind of smear campaign as being from back in the old days. Dirty journalism. Yellow journalism. What do you call it?"

"It still happens."

"On this assignment," Captain Neale said, "I'm learning a lot of things I didn't particularly want to know."

"Is the campaign against me going to continue? Are the March newspapers going to continue to smear me now that Walter March is dead?"

"I understand it's been called off. Mister Williams—Jake Williams—has called it off."

"Good."

"Not for your sake. He thinks it might hurt the image of the recently departed. Leave a bad taste in the mouths of people regarding Walter March."

"If that's their reasoning, I wish they'd continue with it. Walter March tasted like piss and vinegar."

"Interesting to see how decisions are made in the media. You people are feeding a thousand facts and ideas into human minds a day and, I see, sometimes for some pretty wrong reasons."

"Very seldom. It's just that in every woodpile there's a Walter March."

"Anyway, Mister Wisham, Walter March had begun a campaign to destroy you; he was murdered; the campaign was called off."

"Captain Neale, who tipped you?"

"I don't get you."

"Who told you about the editorial, and the campaign?"

"I'm not a journalist, Mister Wisham. I don't have to give my sources—except in a court of law."

"I'll have to wait, uh?"

"I intend to bring this case into court, Mister Wisham. And get a conviction."

"Why did you say that?"

"What do you mean?"

"Seems a funny thing for you to say. I mean, of course you intend to bring it into court. There was a murder. You're a cop."

"Well. . . ."

"Could it be that you've heard some not-very-nice things about Walter March?"

"I've been on the case only twenty-four hours."

"Twenty-four hours investigating Walter March would be enough to make anyone puke."

"Mrs. March assures me he hadn't an enemy in the world. And there is the fact that Walter March was the elected President of the American Journalism Alliance."

"Yeah. And Attila led the Huns."

"Mister Wisham, any man with that much power. . . ."

". . . has to have a few enemies. Right. Everyone loved Walter March except anyone who ever had anything to do with him."

"Mister Wisham. . . ."

"I have one more question."

"Mister Wisham, I. . . . I'll ask the questions."

"Have you ever seen me on television?"

"Of course."

"Often?"

"Yes, I guess so. My working hours. . . . I don't have any regular television-viewing hours."

"What do you think of me? What do you think of my work?"

"Well. I'm not a journalist."

"I don't work for journalists. I work for people. You're a people."

"I'm not a critic."

"I don't work for critics, either."

"I find your work very good."

" 'Very good'?"

"Well, I haven't made a study of it, of course. Somehow or other I never thought I'd be asked by Rolly

131

Wisham what I think of his television reporting. Mostly, of course, I look at the sports. . . ."

"Nevertheless. Tell me what you think of my work."

"I think it's very good. I like it. What you do is different from what the others do. Let me see. I have more of a sense of people from your stories. You don't just sit back in a studio and report something. You're in your shirtsleeves, and you're in the street. Whatever you're talking about, dope addicts, petty criminals, you make us see them as people—with their own problems, and fears. I don't know how to judge it as journalism. . . ."

"I wish you were a critic. You just gave me a good review."

"Well, I have no way to judge such things."

"Next question is. . . ."

"No more questions, Mister Wisham."

"If I'm good enough at my job to please you, the network, and a hell of a lot of viewers—how come Walter March was out to screw me?"

"That's a question."

"Got an answer?"

"No. But I've got some questions."

"I'm asking them for you."

"Okay, Mister Wisham. You're more experienced at asking questions than I am. I've got the point."

"That's not the point. I'm not trying to put you down, Captain Neale. I'm trying to tell you something."

"What? What are you trying to tell me?"

"You look at television. There are a lot of television reporters. Most of us have our own style. What's the difference between me and the others? I'm younger than most of them. My hair is a little longer. I don't work in a studio in a jacket and tie. My reports are usually feature stories. They're supposed to be softer than so-called hard news. Most of my stories have to do with people's attitudes, and feelings, more than just hard facts. That's my job, and you just said I do it pretty well."

"Mister Wisham. . . ."

"So, why me? Why would Walter March, or anyone else, raise a national campaign to get me off the air?"

"Okay, Mister Wisham. Rolly. You asked the question. You could wear an elephant down to a mouse."

"Because he was afraid of me."

"Walter March? Afraid of you?"

"I was becoming an enormous threat to him."

"Ah. . . . Someone told me last night—I think it was that Nettie Horn woman—all you journalists have identity problems. 'Delusions of grandeur,' she said. Rolly, a few minutes of network television time a week—I mean, against Walter March and all those newspapers coast-to-coast, coming out every day, edition after edition. . . ."

"Potentially I was an enormous threat to him."

"Okay, Rolly. I'm supposed to ask 'Why?' now. Is that right?"

"I've been trying to tell you something."

"Okay."

"I have more reason to murder that bastard than anyone you can think of."

"Uh. . . ."

"Don't tell me I need a lawyer. I know my rights. I came to this convention because the network forced me to. I came with such hatred for that bastard. . . . Frankly, I was afraid to cross his path, to see him, or even hear him, or be in a room with him—for fear of what I might do to him."

"Wait."

"My Dad owned a newspaper in Denver. I was brought up skiing, horsing around, loving journalism, my Dad, happy to be the son of a newspaper publisher.

133

Once a newspaper starts to decline in popularity, it's almost impossible to reverse the trend. I didn't know it, but when I was about ten, Dad's newspaper began to go into a decline. By the time I was fourteen, he had mortgaged everything, including his desk, Goddamn it, the desk he had inherited from his father, to keep the paper running. These were straight bank loans—but unfortunately Dad had made the mistake of using only one bank. He wasn't the sharpest businessman in the world."

"Neither am I. I. . . ."

"Just when Dad thought he was turning the paper around—it had taken five years—this one bank called all the loans."

"Could they do that? I mean, legally?"

"Sure. Dad never thought they would. They were friends. He went to see them. They wouldn't even speak to him. They called all the loans at once, and that was it."

"I don't get it."

"Neither did Dad. Why would the bank want to take over a newspaper, especially when there was hope for its doing well? They wouldn't know how to run it. Dad lost the newspaper. He gave up as decently as he could. He wandered around the house for weeks, trying to figure out what had happened. I was fifteen. There was a rumor around that the bank had sold the newspaper to Walter March, of March Newspapers."

"Okay, it seems like an ordinary. . . ."

"Not a bit ordinary. These bankers were old friends of my father. Huntin', fishin', cussin' and drinkin' friends."

"He was hurt."

"He was curious. He was also a hell of a journalist. In time, he found out what happened. People always talk. Walter March had bought up Dad's loans, lock, stock, and barrel—to get control of the newspaper."

"Why did the bankers let him? They were friends. . . ."

"Blackmail, Captain Neale. Sheer, unadulterated blackmail. He had blackmailed the bankers, individually, as persons. So far, in your twenty-four hours of investigation, have you heard about Walter March and his flotilla of private detectives?"

"I've heard rumors."

"When I was sixteen, Dad died of a gunshot wound, in the temple, fired at close range."

The recording tape reel revolved three times before Rolly Wisham said, "I never could understand why Dad didn't shoot Walter March instead."

"Mister Wisham, I really think you should have a lawyer present. . . ."

"No lawyer."

Captain Neale sighed audibly. "Where were you at eight o'clock Monday morning?"

"I had driven into Hendricks to get the newspapers and have breakfast in a drugstore, or whatever I could find."

"You have a car here?"

"A rented car."

"You could have had breakfast and gotten your newspapers here at the hotel."

"I wanted to get out of the hotel. Night before, I had seen Walter March with Jake Williams in the elevator. They were laughing. Something about the President and golf . . . catfish. I hadn't slept all night."

"Did you drive into Hendricks alone?"

"Yes."

"Okay, Mister Wisham, I don't see any problem. Your face is famous. We can just ask people down in the village. I'm sure they saw you, and recognized you. Where did you have breakfast?"

"I never got out of the car, Captain Neale."

"What?"

"I did not have breakfast, and did not buy newspapers. At least, not until I got back to the hotel."

"Oh, Lord."

"I changed my mind. I drove through that shopping center and said, to hell with it. It was a beautiful morning and the shopping center looked so sterile. Also, of course, I'm forever making simple little plans like going to a drugstore for breakfast—I like people, you know? I like being with people—and I get right up to it, and I realize everybody will recognize me, and giggle, and shake hands, and ask for autographs. I'm not keen on that part of my life."

"Are you saying that no one saw you Monday morning?"

"I guess I prevented anyone from seeing me. I wore sunglasses. I drove around. Over the hills. Maybe I was trying to talk myself out of murdering Walter March."

"What time did you leave the hotel?"

"About seven-fifteen."

"What time did you get back?"

"About nine. I had breakfast in the coffee shop here. I didn't hear about Walter March's murder until later. Ten-thirty. Eleven."

"Okay, Mister Wisham. You say Walter March was smearing you, trying to destroy you...."

"Not 'trying to,' Captain Neale. He was going to. There is no doubt in my mind he would have succeeded."

"... because you were becoming a potential threat to him."

"Don't you agree? I could never be as powerful as Walter March. We lost the only newspaper we had. But I have been becoming an increasingly powerful and respected journalist. I'm only twenty-eight, Captain

Neale. I have a lot to say, and a forum for saying it. Even having me at this convention, telling people what I know about Walter March, was a threat to him. You've got to admit, I was more a threat to him as a halfway decent and important journalist than if I had become a skiing instructor in Aspen."

"I guess so. Tell me, Mister Wisham, do you happen to know what suite the March family were in?"

"Suite 3."

"How did you know that?"

"I checked. I wanted to avoid any area in which Walter March might be."

"You checked at the desk?"

"Yup. Which gave me an opportunity to steal the scissors. Right?"

"You're being very open with me, Mister Wisham."

"I'm a very open guy. Anyhow, you strike me as a pretty good cop. There's a lot of pressure on this case. Sooner or later, you'd discover Walter March drove my Dad to suicide. Everyone in Denver knows it, and probably half the people here at the convention do. Concealing evidence against myself would just waste your time, and leave me hung up."

"It's almost as if you were daring me, Mister Wisham."

"I am daring you, Captain Neale. I've worked a lot with cops. I'm daring you to be on my side, and to believe I didn't kill Walter March."

Twenty

COMPUTERS AND LABOR UNIONS
Seminar
Aunt Sally Hendricks Sewing Room

At three-thirty Wednesday afternoon all the tennis courts were in use, the swimming pool area was full, and on the hills around Hendricks Plantation House people were walking and horseback riding.

The bar (Bobby-Joe Hendricks Lounge) was dark and empty except for some people from the Boston press keeping up their luncheon glow with gin and tonics.

And Walter March, Junior, sitting at the bar.

Fletch sat beside him and ordered a gin and bitter lemon from the bored, slow-moving barman.

At the sound of his voice, Junior's head turned slowly to look at him.

Junior's eyes were red-rimmed and glazed, his cheeks puffy, his mouth slack. A small vein in his temple was throbbing. He looked away, slowly, thought a moment, burped, and looked back at Fletch.

He said, "William Morris Fletcher. I remember you."

"Irwin Maurice Fletcher."

"Tha's right. You used to work for us."

"Practically everybody used to work for you."

138

"Flesh. There used to be a joke about you. 'And the Word was made Fletch.'"

"Yeah."

"There were lots of jokes about you. You were a joke."

Fletch paid the barman.

Walter March, Junior, said, "You heard my father's dead?"

"I heard something to that effect."

"Someone stabbed him." Junior made a stabbing motion with his right hand, his eyes looking insane as he did it. "With a scissors."

Fletch said, "Tough to take."

"Tough!" Junior snorted. "Tough for him. Tough for March Newspapers. Tough for the whole motherfuckin' world."

"Tough for you."

"Yeah." Junior blinked slowly. "Tough for me. Tough darts. Isn't that what we used to say in school?"

"I don't know. I wasn't in school with you."

There was a long, slow, blinking pause.

Junior said, "My father hated you."

Fletch said, "Your father hated everybody."

Another three blinks.

"I hated you."

"Anyone who hates me is probably right."

"My Jesus father thought you were night and day."

Fletch sipped his drink. "What does that mean?"

Junior tried to look at Fletch in the proper executive fashion. "You know, he wanted to make a thing with you. He loved your balls." Junior's eyelids drooped. "He wanted to bring you along, you know? Make something of you."

"Gee, and I'm not even in journalism anymore. Just a hanger-on."

"Do you remember his trying to frighten you once?"

139

"No."

"He tried to scare you."

"I don't remember it."

"Tha's because you weren't frightened, shit. You remember the story about the Governor's secretary?"

"Yeah."

"He sent memos to you. Directly. Telling you to blow the story."

"Sure."

"He came to town. Sent for you in his office."

"Yeah."

"Scared the shit out of you."

"Did he?"

"Told you you'd be fired if you wrote the story."

"Five minutes in an office. . . ."

Junior's head swooped up toward Fletch. "You wrote the fuckin' story! And then quit!"

"Yeah."

There was a long pause, and two small burps.

"It wasn't the Governor Dad cared about. Not the Governor's secretary. Not the story." This time Junior put the back of his hand to his burp. "It was you."

"There was a long pause," Irwin Maurice Fletcher said, "while Irwin Maurice Fletcher reacted."

"You don't get the point," Junior said.

"I get the point," Fletch said. "People are always shittin' around, and I'm me. I always get the point."

"Apologize."

"Apologize?"

"Jesus, yes. Apologize."

"For what? For everyone else always shittin' around, or for me being me?"

"Before my Dad did that . . ."—apparently, Junior was considering the prudence of saying what he was about to say—"he had every kind of a fix run on you."

Fletch sat quietly over his drink.

"He wanted you," Junior said.

"I was an employee. I wrote that story. Quit. A common incident, in this business."

"Dad didn't want any of that. He wanted you. He ran every kind of a fix on you. Have I said that?"

"No."

"Before he tried to throw the scare into you, he had you worked over with a fine-toothed . . . pig."

"That I don't understand."

"He wanted you. You were tough. You didn't scare."

"He let me resign."

"That, beaut . . ."—Junior leaned toward him—"was because he hadn't figured you out. He gave up, you see."

"He put detectives on me?"

"He liked your style. In the city room. You were a thousand-dollar job, at first. A mere hand job. He couldn't believe what he found out. More. Ten thousand. Fifteen."

"I would rather have taken it in pay."

"He couldn't believe. . . . Who were you married to then?"

"I don't remember."

"He said, 'Either all of it's true, or none of it's true.'"

"None of it's true," Fletch said. "At the age of eleven, if you want the truth. . . ."

"Stories," Junior said. "Used to get stories about you. At dinner."

Fletch said, "This is very uncomfortable. What a lousy bar. The barman has dirty elbows. No music. What's that noise? 'Moon River.' That's what I mean. No music. Look at that painting. Disgusting. A horse, of all things. A horse over a bar. Ridiculous. . . ."

Junior was blinking over his drink.

"It was me Dad hated."

141

"What?"

"All my life . . . I grew up. . . ."

"Most of us did."

". . . being Walter March, Junior. Walter March Newspapers, Junior. The inheritor of enormous power."

"That can be a problem."

"What if I wanted to be a violinist, or a painter, or a baseball player?"

"Did you?"

Junior closed his eyes tight over his drink.

"I don't even know."

Someone at the table in the corner said, "Walter marched."

Someone else said, "And about time, to boot!"

Fletch looked over at them.

Junior hadn't heard.

"You know, the first day I was supposed to report for work," Junior said. "September. The year I graduated college. They'd let me have the summer off. I walked to the office. Stood across the street from it, staring at it. Twenty minutes. Maybe a half-hour. Then I walked back to my apartment. I was scared shitless. That night, Jake Williams came over to my apartment and talked to me. For hours. Next morning, he picked me up and we walked into the March Newspapers Building together." Junior went through the motions of drinking from his empty glass. "Good old Jake Williams."

Fletch said nothing.

"Fletcher, will you help me?"

"How?"

"Work with me. The way Dad wanted."

"I don't know anything about the publishing side of this business. The business end."

"It doesn't matter."

"It does to me."

Junior tightened his right fist and let it down slowly on the bar, as if he were banging it in slow motion.

"Help me!"

"Junior, I suspect you missed lunch."

"My father loved you so much."

"Come on, I met the bastard—I mean, your father—I mean, your father the bastard, the big bastard five minutes in his office. . . ."

"I can't esplain. I can't esplain."

Fletch, on his bar stool, was facing Walter March, Junior.

There were tears on Junior's cheeks.

Fletch said, "Nappy time?"

Junior straightened up immediately. Suddenly, no tears. No whining voice. No quivering. Princeton right down the spine. Hand firmly around the empty glass. Not deigning to answer.

"Hey, Walt," Fletch said. "I was thinking of a sauna and a rub. They've got this fantastic lady hidden away in the basement, a Mrs. Leary, she gives a great massage. . . ."

Junior looked at him. He was the President of March Newspapers.

"Good to see you again, Fletcher," he said. He cleared his throat. "I guess I just said I'm sorry you didn't stay aboard." He dipped his head to Fletch. "Can I have a drink sent to your room?"

"No, that's all right." Fletch stood up from the bar stool.

He looked at Junior, closely, through the dark of the bar.

"As a matter of fact, Walt." Fletch put his hands in his trouser pockets. "I would like you to send a drink to my room." He drawled, "I'd appreciate it. Room

79." He spoke slowly, softly, deliberately. "A couple of gin and tonics. Room 79. Okay? I'd appreciate it. Room 79."

Fletch wasn't sure how well Junior was hearing him, if at all.

"Thanks, Walt."

Twenty-one

From TAPE
Station 8
Suite 8 (Oscar Perlman)

"... Yeah."

"May I say, Mister Perlman, how much my wife enjoys your columns."

"Fuck your wife."

"Sir?" Captain Neale said.

"Fuck your wife. It's always, 'My wife likes your columns.' " Clearly, Oscar Perlman was talking through a well-chewed cigar. "Everytime I do anything, a book, a play, it's always, 'My wife likes it.' I go to a party and try to get the topic of conversation off me and my work, because I know what to expect all ready. I say, 'What did you think of Nureyev last night at the National Theater?' 'My wife liked it.' Always, 'My wife liked it.' You saw the latest Bergman? 'My wife liked it.' What about Neil Diamond's latest record—isn't it somethin' else? 'My wife liked it.' You read the new Joe Gores novel? 'My wife. . . .' What about *King Lear* these days? 'My wife says it's chauvinistic. The father expects something.' Always, 'My wife liked it, didn't like it.' What are American men, a bunch of cultural shits? Always what the wife likes. The men don't have eyes, ears, and a brain? What'sa matter with you? You can't say you like my column? It's feminine to like my column? Will your chest suck up your hair and push it out your asshole if you say you like something other than hockey, boxing, and other nose-endangering sports?"

"Mister Perlman, I am just a normal veteran. . . ."

"You do fuck your wife, don't you?"

"I have never met such a bunch of strange, eccentric, maybe sick people. . . ."

"Does she say she likes it?"

"Mister Perlman. . . ."

"Do you believe everything your wife says? Who should believe everything his wife says anyway? Why don't you say you enjoy my column? I work just for wives? Fred Waring worked for wives. And look at him. He invented Mixmasters. No, he invented Waring blenders. Maybe there's a man who's pleased to have everybody come up to him saying, 'My wife likes your work.' He sold plenty of Waring blenders. Jesus Christ, why don't you just shut up and sit down.

"I have a terrible feeling I've just blown a column on you," Oscar Perlman said. "So already you owe me seventeen thousand dollars. Relax. You want a cigar? Play cards? A little up and down? I don't drink, but there's plenty stuff around.

"Christ. I just blew a column. How's your wife? I'm supposed to be here enjoying. I'm not. I lost twelve hundred bucks last night. These little shits from Dallas. St. Louis. Oof. Twelve hundred bucks. What? You don't want a drink? These cards are dirty. They took twelve hundred from me."

"Mister Perlman, any time you're ready to answer some questions. . . ."

"Shoot. So old Walter March got it up-the. Never was up-the more deserved. Everybody else 'round here is writing about it. To me, it isn't funny yet. Make it funny for me. I'll appreciate."

"Mister Perlman!"

"Don't shout at me, you backwater, egg-sucking cop. You've cost me a column already. You were a veteran?"

"Listen. I know you journalists are in the business of asking questions. I'm in the business of asking questions. I'm going to ask the questions. Is that clear?"

"Jesus. He's getting hysterical. You don't play cards at all? You should. Very relaxing."

"Mister Perlman, you used to work for Walter March?"

"Years ago. I worked on one of his newspapers. Twenty-five years ago. Most of the people here at this convention worked for March, one time or another. Why ask me?"

"I'm asking the questions."

"That's not a question."

"You first wrote your humorous column on his newspaper?"

"You say it's humorous? Thank you."

"You first developed your column on his newspaper."

"That's not a question, either, but the answer is yes."

"Then you took the column you had developed on one of March's newspapers—the one in Washington—and sold it to a national syndicate?"

"International. Wives all over the world like my column."

"Why did you walk out on Walter March and sell your column to another syndicate?"

"I'm supposed to starve because the man didn't have a sense of humor? Even his wife didn't have a sense of humor. He refused to syndicate my column even through his own newspaper chain. I gave him enough time. Two, three years."

"Is it true he helped you develop your column?"

"Is it true trees grow upside down? 'It's true,' the

dairy maid said, 'if you're always lying on your back.' He allowed the column to run. Irregularly. Usually cut in half. On the obituary page. From his encouragement, I could have had a free funeral, I was so big with the local undertakers."

"And after you went with the syndicate, he sued you, is that true?"

"He didn't win the suit. You can't sue talent."

"But he did sue you."

"You can't sue talent and win. He was laughed out of court. The judge's wife had a sense of humor."

"And then, what?"

Oscar Perlman repeated, "And then, what?"

"Mrs. March says the antagonism between you two has kept up all these years."

"Old Lydia's fingering me, uh? That lady's got sharp nails."

"Has the antagonism between you kept up all these years?"

"How could it? We've had nothing to do with each other. He's been running his newspapers; I've been writing my column."

"Someone told me March never gave up trying to force you to run your column in his newspapers."

"Who told you that?"

"Well, actually, Stuart Poynton."

"Nice guy. Did he get my name right?"

"I was wondering about that. He kept calling you 'Oscar Worldman.' "

"Sounds about right."

"Did you change your name?"

"No. Poynton did. He changes everybody's name. He's a walking justice of the peace."

"Please answer the question, Mister Perlman."

"Did March continue to want my column to run in his newspapers? Well, in most areas, as things worked out, my column ran in newspapers competing with his. I attract a few readers. Yes, I guess the matter would continue to be of some importance to him."

"What was the nature of Walter March's, let's say, effort to get your column back in the March Newspapers."

"You tell me."

"Mister Perlman...."

"No one's pinned anything on me since I was a baby. That's an old line, I'm ashamed to say."

"Are you aware that Walter March kept a large number of private detectives on his payroll?"

"Who told you that?"

"You journalists are mighty particular about pinning down the sources of every statement, aren't you?"

"Who told you?"

"Rolly Wisham, for one."

"Rolly? Nice kid."

"Were you aware of Mister March's private detectives, Mister Perlman?"

"If they were any good as private detectives I wouldn't be aware of them, would I?"

"Did Walter March ever try to blackmail you?"

"How? There's absolutely nothing in my life I could be blackmailed about. My life is as clean as a Minnesota kitchen."

There was a pause.

Stretched out on his bed, Fletch had closed his eyes.

Finally, Captain Neale said, "Where were you Monday morning at eight o'clock?"

"In my bedroom. Sleeping."

"You were in the corridor, outside the March's suite."

"I was not."

"You were seen there."

"I couldn't have been."

"Mister Perlman, Mrs. March has given us a very detailed description of running through the open door of her suite, seeing you in the corridor, walking away, lighting a cigar, running toward you for help, recognizing you, then running past you to bang on the door of the Williams' suite."

"She was upset. She could have seen green zebras at that point."

"You don't remember seeing Lydia March at eight o'clock Monday morning?"

"Not even in my dreams. Captain Neale, we played poker until five-thirty in the morning. I slept until eleven, eleven-thirty."

"Is there anyone here you know of Mrs. March could confuse with you?"

"Robert Redford didn't come to this convention."

"You're willing to swear you were not in the corridor outside the March's suite about eight o'clock Monday morning?"

"Lydia March would be a totally unreliable witness about what or whom she saw at that moment in time."

"Is that what you're relying on, Mister Perlman?"

"You want to know who killed Walter March? I'll tell you who killed Walter March. Stuart Poynton killed Walter March. He was trying to kill Lewis Graham, only he got the names and room numbers mixed up."

Twenty-two

4:30 P.M.

THE BIG I: ADVOCACY JOURNALISM—
RIGHT OR WRONG AND WHO SAYS SO?
Seminar
Conservatory

Fletch was kneeling, shoving his marvelous machine back under the bed, when he heard the glass door to the pool area slide open.

He dropped the edge of the bedspread to the floor.

He hadn't realized the sliding glass door was unlocked.

He heard Crystal's voice. "Now I've got the Fletch story to cap all Fletch stories! Tousle-headed Fletch kneeling by his bed, lisping, 'Now I lay me down with sheep'!"

Crystal was in the doorway, her fat twice banded by a black bikini.

"I met a Methodist minister on the airplane the other day." He stood up. "Twelve thousand meters up he taught me to sing 'Nearer, My God, to Thee.' "

He had never seen so much restrained by so little before.

"I'm cold," she said. "My room's way the other side of the hotel. May I use your shower?"

"Of course."

151

Her skin was beautiful. All of it.

Walking across the room her fat shook so it looked as if it would plop to the floor in handsful.

"That idiot, Stuart Poynton," she said. "Had me standing waist-deep in the pool a half-hour, talking, trying to get me to do legwork for him."

"Legwork?"

"On the Walter March murder. Someone told Poynton I'm unemployed."

She left the bathroom door open.

"Did you agree?"

"I told him I'd work for *Pravda* first."

"Why did you listen?"

Nude, she was adjusting the shower curtain. Even reaching up, her belly hung down.

"Find out if he knew anything. He had some big story about the desk clerk being afraid March was going to get him fired for being rude to Mrs. March, so he grabbed the desk scissors, let himself into March's suite with the master key, and ventilated Walter March as he stood."

Fletch said, "Where does Poynton get stupid stories like that?"

Crystal stepped into the tub, behind the shower curtain.

"Oh, well," he said.

Fletch stripped and went into the bathroom.

He held the shower curtain aside and said, "Room for two of us in here? Watch where you step."

Under the shower, Crystal's body created the most remarkable cascade.

"Did you bring a sandwich?" she asked. "Anything to eat?"

"Young lady, if it's the last thing I do—and it may be—I am going to teach you to not make disparaging remarks about yourself."

"Nothing to eat, uh?"

"I didn't say that."

"Oh, I've never gone for these high-protein diets."

"Obviously. Repeat after me. I will never insult myself again."

" 'I will never insult . . .' yipes!"

When they fell sideways out of the tub, the shower curtain and the bar holding it came with them.

On the bathroom floor, they tried to unwrap themselves from the shower curtain. Part of it was under them, on the floor.

"Goddamn it," he said. "You're on my leg. My left leg!"

"I don't feel a thing," she said.

"I do! I do! Get off!"

"I can't. The shower curtain. . . ."

"Jesus, will you get off my leg! Christ, I think you broke it."

"What do you mean, I broke it? Men are supposed to take some responsibility for situations like this."

"How can I take responsibility when I'm pinned to the floor?"

"You're no good to me pinned to the floor."

"Will you get off my damned leg?"

"Get the shower curtain off me!"

"How can I get the shower curtain off? I can't move."

The shower curtain was yanked, pulled, lifted off from the top.

Fredericka Arbuthnot stood there in tan culottes and a blouse, shower curtain in hand.

Fletch said, "Oh, hi, Freddie."

"Nice to see you, Fletch. Finally."

"Thanks."

Crystal had rolled off him.

Freddie said, "You make a very noisy neighbor."

She dropped the shower curtain, and left.

Fletch was sitting up, feeling up and down his left leg with his fingers.

Face down on the floor, Crystal said, "Did I break it?"

"You didn't break anything."

"You really turn her on, you know?"

"Who?"

"Freddie."

Fletch said, "A bush in the hand. . . ."

Twenty-three

"Did you have a nice shower?" Freddie asked.

"Thanks for rescuing us. Quite an impasse."

"Oh, any time. Really, Fletch, you ought to wear a whistle around your neck, for situations of that sort."

In the Amanda Hendricks Room, Fletch stood with a Chivas Regal and soda in hand, Freddie with a vodka gimlet.

Since he had entered the room, Leona Hatch had been eyeing him curiously.

"And," asked Freddie, "do you always sing at play?"

"Was I singing?"

"Something of doubtful appropriateness. I believe it was 'Nearer, My God, to Thee.' "

"No, no. For Crystal, I was singing, 'Nearer, *my God!* to thee.' "

"Such a happy child."

Leona Hatch swayed over to Fletch and said, "Don't I know you?"

She would make it to dinner tonight, but just barely.

"My name's Fletcher." He put out his hand. "I. M. Fletcher."

Leona took his hand uncertainly. "I don't recognize

the name," she said. "But I'm sure I know you from somewhere."

"I've never worked in Washington."

"Maybe on one of the presidential campaigns?"

"I've never covered one."

"Funny," she said. "I have the feeling I know you very well."

"You probably do," muttered Freddie. "You probably do."

Don Gibbs and another man appeared behind Leona Hatch.

Gibbs' face was highly flushed.

"Fletcher, old man!"

Almost knocking Leona Hatch over—in fact, knocking her hat askew—Don Gibbs, drink in hand, made a clumsy effort to embrace Fletch's shoulders.

"Ha, ha!" Fletch said. "Ha, ha!"

They remained standing in a circle while Fletch looked into his glass and remained quiet.

Don Gibbs, his face highly decorated with smiles, finally said, "Well, Fletch, aren't you going to introduce us?"

Still looking into his glass, Fletch shrugged. "Oh, I'm sure you all know each other."

He looked up in time to see an odd flicker in Fredericka Arbuthnot's left eye.

Leona was resettling her hat on her head at a completely wrong angle.

"Well, I don't know who they are. Who the hell are they?"

"Oh, Ms. Hatch, I'm sorry," Fletch said. "This is Donald Gibbs. And this is Robert Englehardt. They work for the Central Intelligence Agency. Ms. Leona Hatch."

Gibbs' smile sank down his face, his neck, and disappeared somewhere beneath his shirt collar.

Englehardt, a large man in a loose brown suit, turned white all over his bald head.

Freddie said, "You have the C.I.A. on the brain."

Fletch shrugged again. "And frankly, Ms. Hatch, I have no idea who this young lady is."

Englehardt stepped forward and grabbed Leona's free hand in his paw.

"Delighted to meet you, Ms. Hatch. Mister Gibbs and I are observers at your convention. We're from the Canadian press. We're planning a convention of our own, next year, in Ontario. . . ."

"You don't sound Canadian," she said.

"Pip," said Gibbs. "Pip, pip, pip."

"Pop," said Fletch. "Pup."

"See what I mean?" asked Leona. "Since when have Canadians said 'pip'?"

Englehardt, the top of his bald head dampish, gave Fletch a killing look.

"And you pronounced the word 'observers' wrong, too." Leona Hatch shook her arm. "Mister, you're hurting my hand."

"Oh, I'm sorry."

Englehardt not only released her hand, but, in doing so, took a step backward, thus tipping Leona Hatch a little forward.

This time, she caught herself.

She said, "A Canadian would have said, 'I *am* sorry,' with the stress on the *'am.'* A Canadian never would have contracted *'I'* and *'am'* in that sentence under those circumstances."

Don Gibbs had taken several steps backward. He continued to look as if tons of lava were flowing toward him.

Freddie said, "Ms. Hatch, I'm Fredericka Arbuthnot. I work for *Newsworld* magazine."

"Nonsense," sniffed Leona. "No one works for *Newsworld* magazine."

"Ah, here's the beautiful young couple!" Arms extended to embrace the whole world, Helena Williams entered the group. "Hello, Leona. Everything all right?"

Helena looked at Gibbs and Englehardt curiously.

They took several more steps backward.

"Fletch and uh. . . ." She was looking at Freddie. "I forget your name."

"So does she," said Fletch.

"Fredericka Arbuthnot," she said. "For short, you may call me Ms. Blake."

"You know, Leona, I offered these young people the Bridal Suite. But they insist they're not married! What's the world coming to?"

"Great improvement," said Leona Hatch. "Great improvement."

Fletch said, "Helena, I haven't seen Jake around much."

"Well, you know. He's trying to spend as much time with Junior as he can. And with Walter gone. . . . Well, someone has to make the decisions. Junior isn't quite up to it yet." She gave the back of her hair a push. "I'm afraid Jake isn't enjoying this convention, much. None of us is, I suppose."

"In case I don't see Jake, be sure and say hello to him for me," Fletch said.

Helena put her arms out again, to flap to another group. "I surely will, Fletch."

There was a hoarse whisper in Fletch's right ear. "What the hell do you think you're doing?"

Fletch turned, to face Don Gibbs and Robert Englehardt.

He said, "Have you ever tried to lie to someone like Leona Hatch?"

"She's crocked," Gibbs said.

"Have you ever tried to lie to someone like Leona Hatch—even when she's crocked?"

158

Englehardt was looking exceedingly grim.

"She'd pin your wings to a board in one minute flat," Fletch said. "In fact, if you noticed, that's exactly what she did do."

Crystal Faoni came through a crowd to them, casting quite a bow wave.

"Ms. Crystal Faoni," Fletch intoned, "allow me to introduce you to Mister Robert Englehardt and Mister Donald Gibbs, both of the Central Intelligence Agency."

Englehardt's eyes closed and opened slowly.

Gibbs' sweaty upper lip was quivering.

Crystal said, "Hi." She turned to Fletch. "I stayed in my room to watch Lewis Graham on the evening news show. You know what he did?"

"You tell me."

"He did a ninety-second editorial on the theme that people should retire when they say they're going to, regardless of how much they have to give up, using Walter March as an example."

"We wrote that for him at lunch," Fletch said. "I think we can say we contributed to it."

"Did he use the same biblical quotes?"

"Identical."

"Well," said Fletch, "at least one always knows Lewis Graham's sources. May I escort you to the dining room, Ms. Faoni?"

"Oh, goody! Will we be the first ones there? I so like having a perfect record, at the things I do."

"Ms. Faoni," Fletch said, crossing through the cocktail party, her arm in his. "I've just figured something out."

"Who murdered Walter March?"

"Something much more important than that."

"What could be more important than that?"

"The reverse. Death in the presence of life; life in the presence of death."

Crystal said, "Funny the way riddles have always made me hungry."

"Crystal, darling, this afternoon you were trying to get pregnant."

Immediately, she said, "Think we succeeded?"

"Oh, Lord."

"If you remember, I always was very good at math."

They were in the dining room.

"Crystal, sit down."

"Oh, nice. He's taking care of me already." She sat in the chair he held out for her. "Not to worry, Fletcher."

"I promise."

"There's just no way I can be unemployed nine months from now. Good heavens! I'd starve!"

He was sitting next to her, at the empty, round table. "Crystal, you lost a job before, this way. It's an unfair world. You said yourself nothing has changed."

"Oh, yes, it has," she said. "Walter March is dead."

Twenty-four

7:30 P.M. Dinner
Main Dining Room

"Frankly, I think you're all being dreadfully unfair." Eleanor Earles put her napkin next to her coffee cup. "I've never heard so many spiteful, vicious remarks about one man in all my life as I've heard about Walter March since coming here to Hendricks Plantation."

Fletch was at the round table for six with three women—Eleanor Earles, Crystal Faoni, and, of course, Freddie Arbuthnot. No Robert McConnell. No Lewis Graham.

"You all act and talk like a bunch of nasty children in a reformatory, gloating because the biggest boy among you got knifed, rather than like responsible, concerned journalists and human beings."

Crystal burped.

"What have we said?" asked Freddie.

In fact, their conversation had been fairly neutral, mostly concerning the arrival of the Vice-President of the United States the next afternoon, discussing who would play golf with him (Tom Lockhart, Richard Baldridge, and Sheldon Levi; Oscar Perlman had invited him to a strip poker party to prove he had nothing to hide) and whether his most attractive wife would accompany him.

Freddie had just mentioned the memorial service for Walter March to be held in Hendricks the next morning.

"Oh, it's not you." Eleanor looked resentfully around the dining room. "It's all these other twerps."

Eleanor Earles was a highly paid network newsperson, attractive enough, but resented by many because she had done commercials while working for another network—which most journalists refused to do—and, despite that, now had one of the best jobs in the industry.

Many felt she would not have been able to overcome her background and be so elevated if she had not been seized upon by the networks as their token woman.

Nevertheless, she was extremely able.

"Walter March," she said, "was an extraordinary journalist, an extraordinary publisher, and an extraordinary human being."

"He was extraordinary all right," Crystal said into her parfait.

"He had a great sense of news, of the human story, of trends, how to handle a story. His editorial sense was almost flawless. And when March Newspapers came out for or against something, it was seldom wrong. I doubt Walter March was ever wrong."

"Oh, come now," Fletch said.

"What about the way he handled people?" Crystal asked. "What about the way he treated his own employees?"

"Let me tell you," Eleanor said. "I would have considered it a privilege to work for Walter March. Any time, any place, under any circumstances."

"You never worked for him," Crystal said.

Eleanor said, "You know about the time I was stuck in Albania—when I was working for the other network?"

Fletch remembered, vaguely, an incident several

years before—one of those three-day wonder stories—concerning Eleanor Earles in a foreign land. He was a teenager when it happened. It was the first he had ever heard of Eleanor Earles.

"It was just one of those terribly frightening things." Eleanor sat forward, her hands folded slightly below her chin. "I and a producer, Sarah Pulling, had spent five days in Albania, shooting one of those in-country, documentary-type features for the network. Needless to say, we'd had to use an Albanian film crew, and, needless to say, we could film only what they wanted us to, when they wanted us to, and how they wanted us to. However, getting any film, any story out of Albania was considered a coup; it had taken months of diplomatic back-and-forth. Of course they had to accept me as an on-camera person, and I figured if I kept my eyes and ears open I'd be able to add plenty of material and additional comments to the sound track once we got back to New York.

"Despite their ordering us this way and that and putting us up in their best hotel, which had the ambience of a chicken coop, I think they tried to be kind to us. They offered us so much food and drink so continuously, Sarah said she was sure it was their way of preventing us from doing any work at all.

"So things went along fairly well, under the circumstances. We hadn't much control over what we had on film, but we knew we had something.

"The night we were leaving, we packed up and were driven to the airport by some of the people who had been assigned to be our hosts and work with us. It was all very jolly. There were even hugs and kisses at the airport before they left us to wait for the plane.

"Then we were arrested.

"After we had gone through all the formalities of leaving Albania, most of which we didn't even understand, and were actually at the gate, ready to board, two men approached us, took us out of the line, said nothing until everyone else had passed us boarding the plane, until all the airlines personnel had gone about other business—all those eyes carefully averted from the two American women standing silent and somewhat scared with two Albanian bulldogs.

"After everyone had left, they took us by our elbows, marched us through the airport, and into a waiting car.

"We were brought back into the city, stripped, searched, dressed in sort of short, loose cotton house-dress kinds of things that allowed us to freeze, and put in individual, rank, filthy jail cells. Fed those things that look like whole wheat biscuits in pans of cold water, three a day, for three days. No one official ever saw us. No one spoke to us. We were never questioned. Our protests and efforts to get help, get something official happening, got us nowhere. The people who brought us our biscuits and removed our pails just shrugged and smiled sweetly.

"Three days of this. Have you ever been in such circumstances? It's an unreasonable thing. And you find yourself reasoning if they can do it for a day, they can do it for a month. Two days, why not a year? Three days, why not keep you in jail the rest of your life?

"I was sure the network would be yelling at the State Department, and the State Department doing whatever one does under such circumstances and, yes, all that was happening. It was a big news item in the United States and Europe. The network made plenty of hay out of it. They pulled their hair and gnashed their teeth on camera; they made life miserable for several people at the State Department. However, they didn't do whatever was necessary under the circumstances to get us out of jail.

"The afternoon of the fourth day, two men showed up in the corridor between Sarah's and my cells. One of them was an Albanian national. The other was the chief of the Rome bureau of March Newspapers. You know what he said? He said, 'How're ya doin'?'

"Someone unlocked our cells. The two men walked us out of the building, without a word to anyone, and put us, shivering, filthy, stinking into the backseat of a car.

"At the airport the two men shook hands.

"The March Newspapers bureau chief sat in the seat behind us, on the way to Rome, never saying a word.

"At the airport in Rome, all the other passengers were steered into Customs. An Italian policeman took the three of us through a different door, into a reception area, and there, seated in one chair, working from an open briefcase in another chair, was Walter March.

"I had never met him before.

"He glanced up when we came in, got up slowly, closed his briefcase, took it in one hand, and said, 'All right?'

"He drove us into a hotel in Rome, made sure we were checked in, saw us to a suite, and then left us.

"An hour later, we were overcome by our own network people.

"He must have called them, and told them where we were.

"I didn't see Walter March again for years. I sent him many full messages of gratitude, I can tell you, but I was never sure if any got through to him. I never had a response.

"When I finally did meet him, at a reception in Berlin, you know what he said? He said, 'What? Someone was impersonating me in Rome? That happens.' "

Freddie said, "Nice story."

Crystal said, "It brings a tear to my eye."

"Saintly old Walter March," Fletch said. "I've got to go, if you'll all excuse me."

During dinner he had received a note, delivered by a bellman, written on hotel stationery, with *Mr. I. Fletcher* on the envelope, which read: "Dear Fletch— Didn't realize you were here until I saw your name in McConnell's piece in today's Washington paper. Please come see me as soon after dinner as you can—Suite 12. Lydia March."

He had shown the note to no one. (Crystal had expressed curiosity by saying, "For someone unemployed, you sure get interrupted at meals a lot. No wonder you're slim. When you're working, you must never get to eat.")

Eleanor Earles said, "I take it you've worked for Walter March?"

"I have," said Crystal.

"I have," said Fletch.

Freddie smiled, and said, "No."

"And he was tough on you?" Eleanor asked.

"No," said Crystal. "He was rotten to me."

Fletch said nothing.

Eleanor said, to both of them, "I suspect you deserved it."

Twenty-five

THERE'S A TIME AND A PLACE FOR HUMOR:
WASHINGTON, NOW
Address by Oscar Perlman

The door to Suite 12 was opened to Fletch by Jake Williams, notebook and pen in hand, looking drawn and harassed.

"Fletcher!"

They shook hands warmly.

Lydia, in a pearl-gray house gown, was standing across the living room, several long pieces of yellow Teletype paper in one hand, reading glasses in the other.

Her pale blue eyes summed up Fletch very quickly and not unkindly.

"Nice to see you again, Fletch," she said.

Fletch was entirely sure they had never met before.

"We'll be through in one minute," she said. "Just some things Jake has to get off tonight." Leaving Fletch standing there, she put her glasses on her nose and began working through the Teletype sheets, talking to Jake. "I don't see any reason why we have to run this San Francisco story from A.P. Can't our own people in San Francisco work up a story for ourselves?"

"It's a matter of time," Jake said, making a note.

"Poo," said Lydia. "The story isn't going to die in six hours."

"Six hours?"

"If our people can't come up with our own story on this within six hours, then we need some new staff in San Francisco, Jake."

"Mrs. March?" Fletch said.

She looked at him over the frame of her glasses.

"May I use your john?"

"Of course." She pointed with her glasses. "You have to go through the bedroom."

"Thank you."

When he came back to the living room she was sitting on the divan, demitasse service on the coffee table in front of her, not a piece of paper, not even her glasses, in sight.

She said, "Sit down, Fletch."

He sat in a chair across the coffee table from her.

"Has Jake left?"

"Yes. He has a lot to do. Would you care for some coffee?"

"I don't use it."

He was wondering if his marvelous machine was picking up their conversation. He supposed it was.

He wondered what Mrs. March would say if he began singing Gordon Lightfoot's "The Wreck of the *Edmund Fitzgerald*," as he had promised the machine he would.

"Fletch, I understand you're not working."

She was pouring herself coffee.

"On a book."

"Oh, yes," she said. "The journalist's pride. Whenever a journalist hasn't got a job, he says he's working on a book. How many times have I heard it? Sometimes, of course, he is. What's keeping the wolf from the door?"

"My ugly disposition."

She smiled, slightly. "I've heard so much about you,

from one source or another. You were one of my husband's favorite people. He loved to tell stories about you."

"I understand people like to tell outrageous stories about me. I've heard one only lately. Highly imaginative."

"I think you and my husband were very much alike."

"Mrs. March, I met with your husband for five minutes one day, in his office. It was not a successful meeting, for either of us."

"Of course not. You were too much alike. He had a lot of brashness, you know. Whenever he was presented with alternatives, he always thought up some third course of action no one else had considered. That's about what you do, isn't it?"

Instead of saying "Yes" or "No," Fletch said, "Maybe."

"My point is this, Fletch. Walter is dead."

"I'm sorry I didn't say you have my sympathy."

"Thank you. March Newspapers will need a lot of help. Everything now falls on Junior's shoulders. He's every bit the man his father was, of course, even better, in many ways, but. . . ." She fitted her coffee cup to its saucer. ". . . This death, this murder. . . ."

"It must be a great shock to Junior."

"He's lived so much in his father's. . . . They were great friends."

"Mrs. March, I'm a working stiff. I'm a reporter. I know how to get a story and maybe how to write it. In a pinch I can work on a copydesk. I know a good layout when I see one. I know nothing about the publishing side of this business, how you attract advertising and what it costs per line, how you finance a newspaper, buy machinery. . . ."

"Junior does. He's really very good at the back room mechanics of this business." She poured herself more coffee. "Fletch, this is very much a horse-and-wagon sort of business. The horse has to be in front of the wagon. What a newspaper looks like and how it reads is the horse, and the wagon it pulls is the advertising and whatnot. If a newspaper isn't exciting and important, you can have all the clever people in the world in the back room and it won't work out as a business."

"There's Jake Williams. . . ."

"Oh, Jake." She let her hand flop, in disparagement. "Jake is sort of old, and worn-out."

Jake Williams was a good twenty years younger than Lydia March.

"What I'm asking you, Fletch is: would you help Junior out? He has a terribly tough row to hoe just now. . . ."

"I doubt he'd want me to."

"Why do you say that?"

"I bumped into him in the bar this afternoon, and we had a little chat."

"The bar, the bar!" Her face was annoyed and pained. "Really, Junior's got to pull up his socks, and very soon."

"He seems to have some ambivalent feelings toward me."

"Junior doesn't know what he feels at the moment. He's keeping himself as drunk as he can. To be frank, I suppose a little bit of that is understandable, under the circumstances. But, really, becoming totally inoperable. . . ."

"I think he's afraid."

Her eyes opened wide. "Afraid?"

"I never really had a sense of how much your husband was doing—and how he was doing it—until I came to this convention and started hearing the gossip. Your husband's death was pretty ugly."

Lydia fitted her back into the corner of the divan and stared at the floor.

The lady had much to think about.

"Mrs. March, more than five years ago, your husband announced his retirement. Publicly. All the newspapers carried it. Why didn't he retire?"

"Oh, you heard Lewis Graham tonight. On television."

"I heard about it."

"What a pompous ass. You know, he ran against my husband last year for the presidency of the A.J.A. So he takes all the resentment and hatred he has for my husband, and turns it into ninety seconds of philosophical network pablum."

"Why didn't your husband retire when he said he was going to?"

"You don't know?"

"No."

She was sitting up, looking uneasy. "It was because of that stupid union thing Junior did."

Fletch said, "I still don't know."

"Well, a huge union negotiation was coming up, and Junior thought he'd be clever. Our board of directors had been putting pressure on him for some years, you know, saying they thought he had led too sheltered a life, was too naive. They thought all he wanted was to do his day's work and go home at five o'clock to his wife. Of course, that was before she left him. They insisted he travel more, and, of course he did take that trip to the Far East. . . ."

Fletch remembered that Junior had filed a dispatch from Hong Kong which began, "There are a lot of Chinese . . . ," and every March newspaper printed it on the front page, faithfully, just to make the son of the publisher look ridiculous, which he did.

". . . So I guess Junior wanted to show his father and

the board of directors that he had some ideas of his own, could operate in what he thought was a manly manner. Even Walter, my husband, thought the negotiations were going too smoothly. Even points brought up by our side as negotiating points were being accepted, almost without discussion. Of course, some of the union members smelled a rat and began nosing around. Don't you know about this? Walter did his best to keep it quiet. I guess he succeeded. It was discovered that Junior had invested in a large bar-restaurant with the president of the labor union. Well, he had advanced the man the down payment and had accepted a first and second mortage on the place. Obviously, the union president hadn't contributed a damn thing. Junior thought it was all right, because he had done it out of personal money, not company funds. There was hell to pay, of course. The National Labor Relations Board got involved. There was talk of sending both Junior and the union man to jail. We lost one newspaper because of it—the one in Baltimore. There was no question Walter could leave under such circumstances. And, of course, a thing like that takes years to settle down."

Fletch's inner ear heard Lydia say, *He's every bit the man his father was, of course, even better, in many ways. . . .*

"We're all entitled to one mistake," Lydia said. "Junior's was a beaut. You see, Fletch, it was really the fault of the board of directors, for doubting Junior so. He felt he had to prove something. You do understand that, don't you, Fletch? You see, I think Junior needs a special kind of help. . . ."

Again, Lydia was sitting back on the divan, staring at the floor, clearly a very troubled person.

"Mrs. March, I think you and I should talk again, in a day or two. . . ."

"Yes, of course." With dignity, she stood up and put

out her hand. "Of course, it is now when Junior most needs the help. . . ."

"Yes," Fletch said.

"And in reference to what you said"—Lydia continued to hold his hand—"Junior and I did speak about you tonight, at dinner. He agrees with me. He would like to see you involved in March Newspapers. I wish you'd talk with him more about it. When you can."

"Okay."

At the door, she said, "Thanks for coming up, Fletch. I'm sure you didn't mind missing Oscar Perlman's after-dinner speech. Think of the people down there in the dining room, laughing at that dreadful man. . . ."

Twenty-six

10:00 P.M.
> WOMEN IN JOURNALISM: Face It, Fellas—
> Few Stories Take Nine Months to Finish
> Group Discussion
> *Aunt Sally Hendricks Sewing Room*

From TAPE
Station 4
Suite 9 (Eleanor Earles)

Eleanor Earles was saying, "... Thought I'd go to bed."

"I brought champagne."

"That's nice of you, Rolly, but really, it is late."

"Since when is ten o'clock late?" asked Rolly Wisham. "You're showing your age, Eleanor."

"You know I just got back from Pakistan Sunday."

"No, I didn't know."

"I did."

"How are things in Pakistan?"

"Just dreadful."

"Things are always dreadful in Pakistan."

"Rolly, what do you want?"

"What do you think I want? When a man comes calling at ten o'clock at night, bearing a bottle of champagne. ..."

"A very young man."

"Eleanor, darling, 'This is Rolly Wisham, with love. ...' "

"Very funny, you phony."

"Eleanor. You're forgetting Vienna."

"I'm not forgetting Vienna, Rolly. That was very nice."

"It was raining."

"Rain somehow turns me on."

"Shall I run the shower?"

"Honestly, Rolly! Look, I'm tired, and I'm upset about Walter. . . ."

"Big, great Walter March. Sprung you for bail once, in Albania. And what have you been doing for him ever since?"

"Knock it off, twerp."

"How come everyone in the world is a twerp? Except one old bastard named Walter March?"

"Okay, Rolly, I know you've got all kinds of resentments against Walter because of what happened to your dad's newspaper, and all."

"Not resentment, Eleanor. He killed my father. Can you understand? Killed him. He didn't make the rest of my mother's life any string symphony, either. Or mine. The word 'resentment' is an insult, Eleanor."

"It all happened a long time ago, in Oklahoma. . . ."

"Colorado."

". . . And you know only your side of the story. . . ."

"I have the facts, Eleanor."

"If you have facts, Rolly, why didn't you ever go to court with them? Why haven't you ever printed the facts?"

"I was a kid, Eleanor."

"You've had plenty of time."

"I'll print the facts. One day. You'd better believe it. Shall I open the champagne?"

"No."

"Oh, come on, Eleanor. The old bastard's dead."

"Did you kill him, Rolly?"

175

"Did I murder Walter March?"

"That's the question. If you want to be intimate with me, you can answer an intimate question."

"The question you asked was: Did I murder Walter March?"

"That's the question. What's the answer?"

"The answer is: maybe." There was the pop of the champagne bottle cork, and the immediate sound of it's being poured.

"Really, Rolly."

"Here's to your continued health, Eleanor, your success, and your love life."

"You don't take a hint very easily."

"Not bad champagne. For domestic."

"What is it you really want, Rolly? We can't duplicate Vienna in the rain in Hendricks, Virginia, with an air conditioner blasting."

"Let's talk about Albania."

"That's even worse. I don't like to talk about Albania."

"But you do. You talk about Albania quite a lot."

"Well, it made me famous, that incident. You know that. The network took damn good care of me after that. And damn well they should have. The twerps."

"I've never believed your story about Albania, Eleanor. Sorry. Journalistic skepticism. I'm a good journalist. Fact, I just got a good review from a people. More champagne? Suddenly you're being strangely unresponsive."

"I haven't anything to say."

"You mean, you haven't anything you've ever said."

"You came here to find out something. Right, Rolly? You came here for a story. Rolly Wisham, with love and a bottle of champagne. Well, there is no story, Rolly."

"Yes, there is, Eleanor. I wish you'd stop denying it.

You've told the story so often, attributing what Walter March did for you to Walter March's goodness, you've blinded everybody to the simple, glaring fact that Walter March wasn't any good. He was a prick."

"Even a prick can do one or two good things, Rolly."

"Eleanor, I think you've just admitted something. I suspect I picked a fortunate metaphor."

"Get out of here, Rolly."

"Walter March had to have some reason for springing you out of Albania. He sent his own man in. His Rome bureau chief. You know what it must have cost him. Yet he never took credit for it. He didn't even scoop the story. He let our old network take the credit. Come on, Eleanor."

"Rolly. I'm going to say this once. If you don't get out of here, I'm going to call the police."

"The Hendricks, Virginia, police?"

"House security."

"Come on, Eleanor. Tell old Rolly."

"Jesus, I wish Walter had lived. He would have nailed you to the wall."

"Yes," Rolly Wisham said. "He would have. But he can't now. Can he, Eleanor? There are a lot of things he can't do now. Aren't there, Eleanor?"

A phone was ringing. Lying on his bed, half-asleep, Fletch wasn't sure whether the phone was ringing in Eleanor Earles' room, or his own.

"You're. . . ."

"Shall I leave the champagne?"

"You know what to do with it."

"Good night, Eleanor."

It was Fletch's own phone ringing.

Twenty-seven

"Ye Olde Listening Poste," Fletch said.

He had sat up, on the edge of his bed, and thrown the switch on the marvelous machine before answering the phone.

"Hell, I've been trying to get you all night."

"You succeeded. Are you calling from Boston?"

How many hours, days, weeks, months of his life in total had Fletch had to listen to this man's voice on the phone?

"I've never known a switchboard to be so damned screwed up," Jack Saunders said. "It's easier to get through to the White House during a national emergency."

"There's a convention going on here. And the poor women on the switchboard have to work from only one room information sheet. Are you at the *Star?*"

Jack had been Fletch's city editor for more than a year at a newspaper in Chicago.

More recently, they had met in Boston, where Jack was working as night city editor for the *Star*.

Fletch had even done Jack the minor favor of working a desk for him one night in Boston during an arsonist's binge.

"Of course I'm at the *Star*. Would I be home with my god-awful wife if I could help it?"

"Ah," Fletch said. "The Continuing Romance of Jack and Daphne Saunders. How is the old dear?"

"Fatter, meaner, and uglier than ever."

"Don't knock fat."

"How can you?"

"Got her eyelashes stuck in a freezer's door lately?"

"No, but she plumped into a door the other night. Got the door knob stuck in her belly button. Had to have it surgically removed." Fletch thought Jack remained married to Daphne simply to make up rotten stories about her. "I saw in the Washington newspaper you're at the convention. Working for anyone?"

"Just the C.I.A."

"Yeah. I bet. If you're at a convention, you must be looking for a job. What's the matter? Blow all that money you ripped off?"

"No, but I'm about to."

"I figure you can give me some background on the Walter March murder."

"You mean the *Star* doesn't have people here at the convention?"

"Two of 'em. But if they weren't perfectly useless, we wouldn't have sent 'em."

"Ah, members of the great sixteen-point-seven percent."

"What?"

"Something a friend said."

"So how about it?"

"How about what?"

"Briefing me."

"Why?"

"How about 'old times' sake' as a reason?"

"So I can win another award and you not even tell me but go accept it yourself and make a nice, humble little speech lauding teamwork?"

Such had actually happened.

Saunders said, "I guess technically that would come under the heading of 'old times' sake'—in this instance."

"If I scoop the story, will you offer me a job?"

"I'll offer you a job anyway."

"That's not what I asked. If you get a scoop on this, will you make with a job?"

"Sure."

"Okay. You want background or gossip at this point?"

"Both."

"Walter March was murdered."

"No foolin'."

"Scissors in the back."

"Next you're going to say he fell down dead."

"You're always rushing ahead, Jack."

"Sorry."

"Take one point at a time."

"'Walter March was murdered.' I've written it down."

"He was murdered here at the convention, where everybody knows him, and a great many people hate him."

"He's the elected president."

"You know that Walter March kept a stable of private detectives on his permanent payroll?"

"Of course I do."

"His use of them has irritated many people—apparently given many people reason to murder him. In fact, if you believe what you hear around here, dear old saintly Walter March was blackmailing everybody this side of Tibet."

"Do you know whom he was blackmailing and why?"

"A few. He's been having Oscar Perlman followed and hounded for years and years now."

"Oscar Perlman? The humorist?"

"Used to work for March. His column got picked up by a syndicate, and has been running in March's competing newspapers ever since."

"That was a thousand years ago."

"Nevertheless, he's been hounding Perlman ever since."

"So why should Perlman stab March at this point, when he hasn't before?"

"I don't know. Maybe March's goons finally came up with something."

"Oscar Perlman," Jack Saunders mused. "That would be an amusing trial. It would make great copy."

"Lydia March says she saw Perlman in the corridor outside their suite immediately after the murder. Walking away."

"Good. Let's stick Perlman. Anything for a laugh."

"None of this is printable, Jack."

"I know that. I'm the editor, remember? Daphne and all those ugly kids of mine to feed."

"Rolly Wisham hated Walter March with a passion. He has reason, I guess, but I think his hatred borders on the uncontrollable."

" 'Rolly Wisham, with love'?"

"The same. He says he was so upset at seeing March in the elevator Sunday night, he didn't sleep all night."

"What's his beef?"

"Wisham says that March, again using his p.i.'s, took the family newspaper away from Rolly's dad, and drove him to suicide."

"True?"

"How do I know? If it is true, it happened at a dangerous age for Rolly—fifteen or sixteen—I forget which. Loves and hatreds run deep in people that age."

"I remember. Did Wisham have the opportunity? You said he was there Sunday night."

"Yeah, and he has no working alibi for Monday

morning. He says he was driving around Virginia, in sunglasses, in a rented car. Didn't even stop at a gas station."

"Funny. 'This is Rolly Wisham, with love, and a scissors in Walter March's back.'"

"You know March was planning a coast-to-coast campaign to get Wisham thrown off the air?"

"Oh, yeah. I read that editorial. It was right. Wisham's a fuckin' idiot. The world's greatest practitioner of the sufferin'-Jesus school of journalism."

"Keep your conservative sentiments to yourself, Saunders. You've been off the street too long."

"Two good suspects. We'll start doing background on them both right away. Anyone else?"

"Remember Crystal Faoni?"

"Crystal? Petite Crystal? The sweetheart of every ice cream store? She used to work with us in Chicago."

"She tells me that once when she was pregnant without benefit of ceremony, March fired her on moral grounds. Crystal had no choice but to abort."

"That bastard. That prude. Walter March was the most self-righteous. . . ."

"Yes and no," Fletch said.

"Well, I'll tell you, Fletch. Crystal has the intelligence and imagination to do murder, and get away with it."

"I know."

"I'd hate to have her as an enemy."

"Me too."

"I shiver at the thought. I'd rather have a boa constrictor in bed with me. This Captain Andrew Neale, who's running this investigation, what do you think of him?"

"He's no Inspector Francis Xavier Flynn."

"Sometimes I think Inspector Francis Xavier Flynn isn't, either."

182

Flynn was the only person working for the Boston Police Department with the rank of Inspector.

"I think Neale's all right," Fletch said. "He's working under enormous pressure here—the press all over the place—trying to interview professional interviewers. He's under time pressure. He can keep us here only another twenty-four hours or so."

"Is there anyone else, Fletch, with motive and opportunity?"

"Probably dozens. Robert McConnell is here."

"McConnell. Oh, yeah. He was what's-his-face's press aide. Wanted to go with him to the White House."

"Yeah. And Daddy March endorsed the other candidate, coast-to-coast, which may have made the difference, gave Bob his job back, and sat him in a corner, where he remains to this day."

"Bob could do it."

"Murder?"

"Very sullen kind of guy anyway. Big sense of injustice. Always too quick to shove back, even when nobody's shoved him."

"I noticed."

"We'll do some b.g. on him, too. Who's this guy Stuart Poynton mentions in tomorrow's column?"

"Poynton mentions someone? The desk clerk?"

"I've got the wire copy here. He mentions someone named Joseph Molinaro."

"Never heard of him. I wonder what his name really is."

"I'll read it to you. 'In the investigation of the Walter March murder, local police will issue a national advisory Thursday that they wish to question Joseph Molinaro, twenty-eight, a Caucasian. It is not known that Molinaro was at the scene of the crime at the time the crime was committed. Andrew Neale, in charge of

183

the investigation, would give no reason for the advisory.' Mean anything to you, Fletch?"

"Yeah. It means Poynton conned some poor slob into doing some legwork for him."

"Fletch, sitting back here in the ivory tower of the *Boston Star*. . . ."

"If that's an ivory tower, I'm a lollipop."

"I can lick you anytime."

"Ho, ho."

"My vast brain keeps turning to Junior."

"As the murderer?"

"Walter March, Junior."

"I doubt it."

"Living under Daddy's thumb all his life. . . ."

"I've talked with him."

"That was a very heavy thumb."

"I don't think Junior's that eager to step into the batter's box, if you get me. Mostly he seems scared."

"Scared he might get caught?"

"He's drinking heavily."

"He's been a self-indulgent drinker for years, now."

"I doubt he could organize himself enough."

"How much organization does it take to put a scissors in your daddy's back?"

Fletch remembered the stabbing motion Junior made, sitting next to him in the bar, and the insane look in his eyes as he did it.

Fletch said, "Maybe. Now, would you like to know who the murderer is?"

Jack Saunders chuckled. "No, thanks."

"No?"

"That night, during the Charlestown fires, you had it figured out the arsonist was a young gas station attendant who worked in a garage at the corner of Breed and Acorn streets and got off work at six o'clock."

"It was a good guess. Well worked-out."

"Only the arsonist was a forty-three-year-old baker deputized by Christ."

"We all goof up once in a while."

"I think I can stand the suspense on this one a little longer."

"Anyway, Christ hadn't told me."

"If you get a story, you'll call me?"

"Sure, Jack, sure. Anything for 'old times' sake.'"

Twenty-eight

From TAPE
Station 5
Suite 3 (Donald Gibbs and Robert Englehardt)

"Snow, beautiful snow!"

From his voice, Fletch guessed Don had had plenty of something.

"Who'd ever expect snow in Virginia this time of year?"

Fletch couldn't make out what Englehardt muttered.

"Who'd ever think my dear old department headie, Bobby Englehardt, would travel through the South with snow in his attaché case? Good thing it didn't melt!"

Another unintelligible mutter from Englehardt.

"Well, I've got a surprise for you, too, dear old department headie," Gibbs said. " 'What's that?' you ask with one voice. Well! I've got a surprise for you! 'Member those two sweet little things in Billy-Bobby's boo-boo-bar lounge? 'Sweet little things,' you say together. Well, sir, I had the piss-pa-cacity to invite them up! To our glorious journalists' suite. This very night! This very hour! This very minute! In fact, for twenty minutes ago."

"You did?"

"I did. Where the hell are they? Got to live like journalists, right? Wild, wild, wicked women! Live it up!"

"I invited someone, too." Englehardt's voice sounded surprisingly cautious.

"You did? We gonna have four broads? Four naked, writhing girls? All in the same room?"

"The lifeguard," Englehardt said.

"The lifeguard? Which lifeguard? The boy lifeguard? There weren't any other type. I looked."

Englehardt muttered something. There was a silence from Gibbs.

Then Englehardt said, "What's the matter, Don? Don't you like a change?"

"Jesus. Two girls and a boy. And us. For a fuck party. An orgy. Bob. . . ."

"Take it calm, Gibbs."

"Where's the bourbon? I want the bourbon. Back of my nose feels funny."

The doorbell in the suite was ringing.

"And the Lord High Mayor ate pomegranates," Don Gibbs said. "Surprising fellas, department heads. Lifeguards with snow on. Boy lifeguards."

". . . Confront new situations," Englehardt said. "Part of your training. Field training."

"Never saw anything about it in the manual."

Englehardt said, "You can do it that way, too."

Fletch's own phone was ringing.

"Hello?"

He had turned the volume down on his machine. It was Freddie Arbuthnot.

"Fletcher, I thought I'd be more subtle. Meet you for a swim? Or have you about had it for today?"

"Are you in your room?"

"Yes."

"Can't you hear my tape recorder?"

"That's how I knew you were still awake."

"Then you should be able to figure out I'm working very hard. On my travel piece."

"By now, I think, you'd have said everything there is to say about Italy."

"You can never say enough about Italy. A gorgeous country filled with gorgeous people. . . ."

"All work and no play. . . ."

"Makes jack."

"Why don't you stop working, and come for a swim? We can have the pool all to ourselves."

"What time is it in your room?"

"Midnight. Twelve-thirty-five. What time is it in yours?"

"My dear young lady. Crystal Faoni got very cold in that pool during the mid-afternoon."

"And with all her insulation."

"She was chilled."

"I saw your efforts to warm her up."

"Now, if she got cold in mid-afternoon, what do you think might happen to us at half-past midnight?"

"We might get warmed up."

"You miss the point, Ms. Arbuthnot."

"The point is, Mister Fletcher, you shot your wad."

"The point is, Ms. Arbuthnot. . . ."

She said, "And I thought you were healthy," and hung up.

There was a poker party, or the poker party, going on in Oscar Perlman's suite, a whacky tobacky party in Sheldon Levi's, silence in the Litwacks'; Leona Hatch was issuing her "Errrrrr's" regularly; Jake Williams was on the phone to a March newspaper in Seattle, sounding very tired (something about how to handle a story about a fistfight among major-league baseball players in a downtown cocktail lounge); in her room Mary McBain appeared to be all alone, crying; Charlie Stieg

188

was in the last stages of a seduction scene with a slightly drunk unknown; Rolly Wisham and Norm Reid were tuned to the same late-night movie in their rooms; Tom Lockhart's room was silent.

Fletch switched back to Station 5, Suite 3.

"Switch!" Don Gibbs was shouting. "Everybody switch! Swish, swish, swish, I SAID!"

There was a considerable variety of background noises, some of which Fletch had difficulty identifying.

A girl's voice sang, "Snow, beautiful snow. . . ."

"Everybody get your snow before it melts," Don Gibbs said.

There was the sound of a hard slap.

Englehardt's voice, low and serious, said, "When I pay money, I want to get what I pay for."

"Cut that out," Gibbs said. "I said, 'Switch!' Everybody switch!"

A young man's voice said, "You're not paying for that, bastard."

"Switch! I said!"

Fletch listened long enough to make sure a second female voice was recorded by his marvelous machine.

Then Don Gibbs was saying, "Whee! We're living like journalists! Goddamn journalists. Goddamn that Fletch! Live like this alla time. Disgusting!"

Fletch put his marvelous machine on automatic, for Station 5, Suite 3, and took a shower.

Twenty-nine

Wednesday

The sun was up enough to have dissipated the dew and, after a long but gentle gallop, make Fletch hot enough to stop and pull off his T-shirt and wrap it around his saddle horn.

When he stopped to do so his eye caught the sun's reflection off a windshield between trees, up the side of a hill, so he rode to a point well behind the vehicle and then up through scrub pine level to it, where he found an old timber road. He rode back along it.

Coming around a curve in the road, he stopped.

A camper was parked in the road.

Behind it, lying on his back, blood coming from his mouth, was the man he had been looking for, the man the masseuse, Mrs. Leary, had mentioned, the man in the blue jeans jacket, the man with the tight, curly gray hair.

He was obviously unconscious.

Over him, on one knee, going through a wallet, now looking up at Fletch apprehensively, was none other than Frank Gillis.

Fletch said, "Good morning."

"Who are you?" Gillis asked.

"Name of Fletcher."

Gillis returned to his investigation of the wallet. "You work here?"

"No."

"What then? Staying at the hotel? Hendricks?"

"Yes."

"You a journalist?" There was a touch of incredulity in Gillis' voice.

"Off and on." Fletch wiped some sweat off his stomach. "You're Frank Gillis."

"You got it first guess."

For years, Frank Gillis had been traveling America finding and reporting those old, usually obscure stories of American history, character, odd incidents, individuals, which spoke of and to the hearts of the American people. During days when America had reason to doubt itself both abroad and at home, Gillis' features were a tonic which made Americans feel better about themselves, even if only for a few minutes, and, probably, during the nation's most trying days, did a lot, in their small way, to hold the nation together.

Fletch said, "And you just mugged somebody."

Gillis stood up and dropped the wallet on the man's chest.

"Yeah, but guess who," he said. "Get down. Come here. Look at him."

Gillis was a man in his fifties, with gentle, smiling eyes and a double chin.

Fletch got off his horse and, holding the reins, walked to where Gillis was standing.

He looked down at the man on the ground.

His was a much younger face than Fletch had expected—much, much younger than indicated by the gray hair.

"My God," Fletch said.

"Right."

"Walter March."

Gillis was looking around at the tops of the trees, fists on his hips, still visibly provoked.

"Why'd you mug him?"

"I have a distinct dislike of people flicking lit cigarettes into my face." He ran his hand over his cheek, left of his nose. "I only hit him once."

"You know him?"

"Don't care to. I stopped to ask for directions." The great explorer of contemporary America smiled sheepishly. "I was lost. This guy was standing here behind the camper, rolling a cigarette. When I saw his face, I was astounded. I said, 'My God, you're the spitting image of . . .' and a real rotten look, real pugnacious, came into his face, so I stopped, and he lit his cigarette, and he said, 'Of who?' and I said, 'Old March, Walter March,' and, flick, the cigarette went into my face and I'd hit him before I knew it." He looked down at the much younger, inert man. "I only hit him once."

"You hit good," Fletch said. "Glad I don't smoke."

"No way to get a story," Gillis said, rubbing his knuckles.

On the ground, the man's head and then his left leg moved.

"What's his name?" Fletch asked.

"Driver's license says Molinaro. Joseph Molinaro. Florida license."

The camper had Florida license plates.

"Golly," said Fletch. "This guy's only twenty-eight years old."

Gillis looked at him sharply, and then said, "Young body. You're probably right."

Suddenly, Molinaro's eyes opened, immediately looking alert and wary, even before shifting to focus on Fletch and Gillis.

"Good morning," Fletch said. "Seems you took a nap before breakfast."

Molinaro sat up on his elbows, and then reacted to pain in his head.

His wallet slipped off his chest onto the dry dirt of the road.

"Take it easy," Fletch said. "You've already missed post time."

Molinaro's eyes glazed and he looked as if he were about to sink to the ground again.

Fletch put his hand behind Molinaro's arm.

"Come on. You'll feel better if you get up. Get the blood going again."

He helped Molinaro stand, waited while he wiped the blood off his lips, examined it on his hand.

Molinaro looked sourly at Gillis.

Throwing off Fletch's hand, Molinaro staggered the few steps to the back of the camper and sat on the sill of the open door.

"You have some bad habits," Gillis said. "And I have a quick temper."

"Your name Joseph Molinaro?" Fletch asked.

The man's eyes moved slowly from Gillis to Fletch without losing any of their bitterness.

He said nothing.

"What relation are you to Walter March?" Gillis asked.

Still the man said nothing.

"Are you his son?" Fletch asked.

The man's eyes lowered to the road, and then off into the scrub pine.

And he snorted.

Fists again on hips, Gillis looked expressionlessly at Fletch.

A mosquito was in the air near Fletch's face. He caught it in his hand.

Gillis went to the side of the road and gathered up his horse's reins and slowly returned to where he had been standing.

He said to Molinaro, "You are Walter March's son. With that face you have to be. Did you murder him?"

Molinaro said, "Why would I murder him?"

"You tell us," Gillis said.

"The son of a bitch is no good to me dead," Molinaro said.

Gillis watched him with narrow eyes, saying nothing.

"What good was he to you alive?" Fletch asked.

Molinaro shrugged. "There was always hope."

There was another silent moment while Molinaro rubbed his temples with the heels of his hands.

Finally, Fletch said, "Come on, Joe. We're not out to get you." He had considered telling Molinaro that Poynton had reported there would be a national advisory issued that morning saying the police wanted to question him. He had also considered advising Captain Andrew Neale of the whereabouts of Joseph Molinaro. "We're not even looking for a story."

Molinaro said, "Just nosy, uh?"

Joseph Molinaro had been in the vicinity of the crime at the time the crime was committed.

He had accosted Mrs. Leary in the parking lot Sunday morning, and Walter March had been murdered Monday morning.

Clearly, Joseph Molinaro was a close relative of Walter March.

Fletch said, "What good was Walter March to you alive?"

"I wrote three or four polite letters when I was fifteen, asking to see him. No answers." Molinaro's fingers

194

were touching his jaw, gently. "When I was nineteen, I took a year's savings, working in a laundry, for Christ's sake, went to New York, lived in a fleabag for as long as I could hold out, just to bug his secretary, asking for an appointment. First I gave my name, then I gave any name I could think of. He was always out of the country, out of the city, in conference." He winced. "I had even bought a suit and tie so I'd have something to dress in, if he'd see me."

"He was your father?" Gillis asked.

"So I've always heard."

"Who told you? Who said so?" Gillis asked.

"My grandparents. They brought me up. In Florida." Molinaro was looking at Gillis with more interest. "I never even saw your fist," he said.

"You never do," said Gillis. "You never see the knockout punch."

"You used to box? I mean, professionally?"

Gillis said, "I used to play piano."

Molinaro shook his head, as much as his head permitted him. "Fat old fart."

"You want to not see my fist again?"

Molinaro stared at him.

"You're Frank Gillis, the television guy."

"I know that," Frank Gillis said.

"I've seen you on television."

"How come you roll your own?" Gillis asked.

"What's it to you?"

"Just unusual. Ever work in the Southwest?"

"Yeah," Molinaro said. "On a dude ranch, in Colorado. And one day I read Walter March owned a Denver newspaper. So I gave up my job and went to Denver and spent every day, all day, outside that newspaper building. Finally, one night, seven o'clock, he came out. Three men with him. I ran up to him. Two of the men blocked me off, big bruisers, the third opened the car door. And off went Walter March."

"Did he see you?" Fletch asked. "Did he see your face?"

"He looked at me before he got into the car. And he looked at me again through the car window as he was being driven off. Three, four years ago. Son of a bitch."

"You know, Joe," Gillis said. "You're not too good at taking a hint."

"What's so wrong with having an illegitimate son?" Molinaro's voice rose. "Jesus! What was ever wrong with it? Even in the Dark Ages, you could say hello to your illegitimate son!"

Standing in the sunlight on a timber road a few kilometers behind Hendricks Plantation, Fletch found himself thinking of Crystal Faoni. *I didn't act contrite enough. . . . He fired a great many people on moral grounds. . . . I'd be pleased to be accused. . . .*

"Your father was sort of screwed up," Fletch said.

Molinaro squinted up at him. "You knew him?"

"I worked for him once. Maybe I spent five minutes in total with him." Fletch said, "Your five minutes, I guess."

Molinaro continued to look at Fletch.

Gillis asked, "You came to Virginia in hopes of seeing him?"

"Yeah."

"How did you know he was here?"

"President of the American Journalism Alliance. The convention. Read about it in the papers. The *Miami Herald*."

"What made you think he'd be any gladder to see you this time than he was last time?"

196

"Older," Molinaro said. "Mellower. There was always hope."

"Why didn't you register at the hotel?" Gillis asked. "Why hide up here in the woods?"

"You kidding? You recognized me. I planned to stay pretty clear of the hotel. Until I absolutely knew I could get through to him."

"Did you contact him at all?" Fletch asked.

"On the radio, Monday night, I heard he'd been murdered. First I knew he'd actually arrived here. I'd been noseying around. Hadn't been able to find out anything."

"Yeah, yeah, yeah," Gillis said. "So why are you still here?"

There was hatred for Gillis on Molinaro's face. "There's a memorial service. This morning. You bastard."

Gillis said, "I'm not the bastard."

He got on his horse and settled her down.

"Hey, Joe," Gillis said. "I'm sorry I said that." The hatred in Molinaro's face did not diminish. "I mean, I'm really sorry."

Fletch said, "Joe. Who was your mother?"

Molinaro gave Fletch the hatred full-face.

And didn't answer.

Fletch stared into the younger, unlined face of Walter March.

He stared into the unmasked hatred.

Having known, slightly, the smooth, controlled, diplomatic mask of Walter March, Fletch was seeing the face now as it probably really was.

Probably as the murderer of Walter March had seen him.

"Joe." Fletch mounted his horse. "Your father was really screwed up. Morally. He made his own laws, and

197

most of 'em stank. Whatever you wanted from your father, I suspect you're better off without."

Sullenly, bitterly, still sitting on the doorsill of the camper, Joseph Molinaro said, "Is that your eulogy?"

"Yeah," Fletch said. "I guess it is."

Thirty

8:00—9:30 A.M. Breakfast
Main Dining Room

The pool was empty, and no one was around it except one man—a very thin man—sitting in a long chair, dressed in baggy, knee-length shorts, a vertically striped shirt open at the throat, and polished black loafers.

Next to his chair was a black attaché case.

Fletch had approached the hotel from the rear, still shirtless and sweaty.

While he was fitting his key into the lock of the sliding glass door, the man came and stood beside him.

He seemed peculiarly interested in seeing the key go into the lock.

"Good morning," Fletch said.

"I.R.S.," the man said.

Fletch slid the door open. "How do you spell that?"

"Internal Revenue Service."

Fletch entered the cool, dark room, leaving the door open.

"Let's see, now, you have something to do with taxes?"

"Something."

He sat on a light chair, the attaché case on his knees.

Fletch threw his T-shirt on the bed, his room key on the bureau.

The man opened the attaché case and appeared ready to proceed.

Fletch said, "You haven't asked me to identify myself."

"Don't need to," the man said. "It appeared in a Washington newspaper you were here. I was sent down. The room clerk said you were in Room 79. You just let yourself in with the key to Room 79."

Fletch said, "Oh. Well, you haven't identified yourself."

The man shook his head. "I.R.S.," he said. "I.R.S."

"But what do I call you?" Fletch asked. "I? I.R.? Mister S.?"

"You don't need to call me anything," I.R.S. said. "Just respond."

"Ir."

Fletch went to the phone and dialed Room 102.

"Calling your lawyer?" I.R.S. asked.

"Crystal?" Fletch said into the phone. "I need a couple of things."

She said, "Have you had breakfast?"

Fletch said, "I forget."

"You forget whether you've had breakfast?"

"I'm not talking about breakfast."

"Was it that bad? I had the pancakes and sausages, myself. Maple syrup. I know I shouldn't have had the blueberry muffins, but I did. It was a long night."

"I know. And you may be eating for two now, right?"

"Fletch, will you ever forgive me?"

"We'll see."

"Good. Then let's do it again."

"I had some difficulty explaining to hotel management how the bar for the shower curtain got ripped out."

"What did you tell them?"

"I told them I tried to do a chin-up."

"They believed that?"

"No. But one has to start one's lying somewhere."

"Were they nasty about it?"

"They were perfectly nice about saying they would put it on my bill. Listen, I need a couple of things. And I have a guest."

"Freddie Arbuthnot? No wonder you forgot breakfast."

Fletch looked at I.R.S. The man was almost entirely Adam's apple.

"Close."

The man's shoulders were little more than outriggers for his ears.

"Anything, Fletcher darling, love of my life. Ask me for anything."

"I need one of those cassette tape recorders. You know, with a tape splicer? I need to splice some tape. Do you have one?"

"Mine doesn't have a splicer. I'm very sure that Bob McConnell has one, though."

"Bob?"

"Would you like me to call him for you?"

"No, thanks. I'll call him myself."

Crystal said, "I think he's disposed to cooperate with you in any way he can."

"Mentioning me in his piece has caused me a little bit of trouble."

I.R.S. was flicking his pen against his thumbnail, impatiently.

"What's the other thing, darling?"

"I finished my travel piece. Want to send it off. Do you have anything like a big envelope, a box, wrapping paper, string?"

"There's a branch post office in the lobby."

"Yeah."

"They sell big mailers these days."

"Oh, yeah."

"Big insulated envelopes, boxes, right up to the legal limit in size."

"Yeah. I forgot."

"Over the door there's a sign saying 'United States Post Office.' "

"Thank you, Crystal."

"If you get lost in the lobby, just ask anyone."

"Crystal? I'm going to say something very, very rotten to you."

"What?"

"The dining room is still open for breakfast."

"Rat."

Fletch hung up but continued standing by the bed. He needed a shower. He thought of jumping in the pool. He wanted to do both.

"If we might get down to the business at hand?" I.R.S. said.

"Oh, yeah. How the hell are ya?"

"Mister Fletcher, our records indicate you've never filed a tax return."

"Gee."

"Are our records accurate?"

"Sure."

"Your various employers over the years—and, I must say, there is an impressive number of them—have withheld tax money from your income, so it's not as if you'd paid no tax at all."

"Good, good."

"However, not filing returns is a crime."

"Shucks."

"As a matter of personal curiosity, may I ask why you have not filed returns?"

"April's always a busy month for me. You know. In the spring a young man's fancy really shouldn't have to turn to the Internal Revenue Service."

"You could always apply for extensions."

"Who has the time to do that?"

"Is there any political thinking behind your not paying taxes?"

"Oh, no. My motives are purely esthetic, if you want to know the truth."

"Esthetic?"

"Yes. I've seen your tax forms. Visually, they're ugly. In fact, very offensive. And their use of the English language is highly objectionable. Perverted."

"Our tax forms are perverted?"

"Ugly and perverted. Just seeing them makes my stomach churn. I know you wallahs have tried to improve them but, if you don't mind my saying so, they're still really dreadful."

I.R.S. blinked. His Adam's apple went up and down like a thermometer in New England.

"Esthetics," he muttered.

"Right."

"All right, Mister Fletcher. We haven't heard from you at all in more than two years. No returns. No applications for extensions."

"Didn't want to bother you."

"Yet our sources indicate you have had an income during this period."

"I'm still alive, thank you. Clearly, I am eating."

"Mister Fletcher, you have money in Brazil, the Bahamas, Switzerland, and Italy."

"You know about Switzerland?"

"Quite a lot of money. Where did you get it?"

"I ripped it off."

" 'Ripped it off'?"

" 'Stole it' seems such a harsh expression."

"You say you stole it?"

"Well, you weren't there at the time."

"I certainly wasn't."

"Maybe you should have been."

"Did you steal the money in this country?"

"Yup."

"How did you get the money out of the country?"

"Flew it out. In a chartered jet."

"My God. That's terribly criminal."

"Why does my not paying taxes and illegally exporting money bother you more than the fact I stole the money in the first place?"

"Really!"

Fletch said, "Just an observation."

Fletch picked up the phone and dialed Room 82.

"Bob? This is your friend Fletcher."

There was a long pause before Robert McConnell said, "Oh, yeah. Hi."

"Crystal tells me you have a cassette tape recorder with a tape splicer attachment."

"Uh. Yes."

"Wonder if I might borrow it for a few hours?"

Robert McConnell was envisioning his sensitive parts tied to a cathedral door if he said no. Dear Crystal.

"Uh. Sure."

"That's great, Bob. You going to be in your room?"

"Yes."

"I'll be by in a few minutes." Fletch started to hang up, but then he said into the receiver, "Bob, I appreciate. Let me buy you a drink."

The only response was a click.

I.R.S. said, "Mister Fletcher, I hope you realize what you've admitted here."

"What's that?"

"That you stole money, illegally exported it from the country, failed to report it as income to the Internal Revenue Service, and have never filed a federal tax return in your life."

"Oh, that. Sure."

"Are you insane?"

"Just esthetic. Those tax forms. . . ."

"Mister Fletcher, you seem to be signing yourself up for a long stretch in prison."

"Yeah. Okay. Make it somewhere South. I really don't like cold weather. Even if I have to be indoors."

There was a knock on his door.

"Have I answered your questions satisfactorily?" Fletch asked.

"For a start." I.R.S. was returning things to his attaché case. "I can't believe my ears."

Fletch opened the door to a bellman.

"Telegrams, sir. Two of them." He handed them over. "You weren't in your room earlier, sir."

"And sliding them under the door, you would have lost your tip. Right?"

The bellman smiled weakly.

"You've lost your tip anyway."

Fletch closed the door before opening the first telegram:

GENERAL KILENDER ARRIVING HENDRICKS FOR BRONZE STAR PRESENTATION MID-AFTERNOON— LETTVIN.

I.R.S. was standing in his droopy drawers, attaché case firmly in hand, staring at Fletch incredulously.

He came toward the door.

The second telegram said:

BOAC FLIGHT 81 WASHINGTON AIRPORT TO LON- DON NINE O'CLOCK TONIGHT RESERVATION YOUR NAME. WILL BE AT BOAC COUNTER SEVEN-THIRTY ON TO RECEIVE TAPES—FABENS AND EGGERS.

At the door, I.R.S. said, "Mister Fletcher, I must order you not to leave Hendricks, not to leave Virginia, and certainly not to leave the United States."

Fletch opened the door for him.

"Wouldn't think of it."

"You'll be hearing from us shortly."

"Always nice doing business with you."

As I.R.S. walked down the corridor, Fletch waved good-bye at him—with the telegrams.

Thirty-one

9:30 A.M.
     PROBLEMS WITH FOREIGN CORRESPONDENCE:
     On Renting a House in Nigeria,
     Finding a School For Your Kids in Singapore,
     Getting a Typewriter Fixed in Spain,
     and Other Problems
     Address by Dixon Hodge
     Conservatory

10:30 A.M.
     WHAT TIME IS IT IN BANGKOK?: An Editor's View
     Address by Cyrus Wood
     Conservatory

[11:00 A.M. Memorial Service for Walter March]
     St. Mary's Church, Hendricks

11:30 A.M.
     THE PLACING OF FOREIGN CORRESPONDENTS:
     Pago Pago's Cheaper, but the Story's in Tokyo
     Address by Horsch Aldrich
     Conservatory

Fletch had a shower, swam a few laps in the pool, dressed, and went to the hotel's writing room, next to the billiards room at the back of the lobby.

On a bookshelf near the fireplace was a copy of *Who's Who in America,* which he pulled down and took to a writing table.

Fletch had learned the habit a long time before of researching the people with whom he was dealing, through whatever resources were within reach.

Sometimes the most simple checking of names and dates could be most revealing:

MARCH, WALTER CODINGTON, publisher; b. Newport, R.I., July 17, 1907; s. Charles Harrison and Mary (Codington) M.; B.A., Princeton, 1929; m. Lydia Bowen, Oct., 1928; 1 son, Walter Codington March, Jr. March Newspapers, 1929–: treas., 1935; vice-pres., corp. affs., 1941; mergers & acquisitions, 1953; pres., 1957; chmn., pub., 1963–. Dir. March Forests, March Trust, Wildflower League. Mem. Princeton C. (N.Y.C.), American Journalism Alliance, Reed Golf (Palm Springs, Ca.), Mattawan Yacht (N.Y.C.), Simonee Yacht (San Francisco). Office: March Building, 12 Codington Pl New York City NY 10008

MARCH, WALTER CODINGTON, JR., newspaperman; b. N.Y.C., Mar. 12, 1929; s. Walter Codington and Lydia (Bowen) AH.: Princeton, 1941. m. Allison Roup, 1956: children—Allison, Lydia, Elizabeth. March Newspapers, 1950–: treas., 1953; vice-pres., corp. affs., 1968; pres., 1973–. Dir. March Forests, March Trust, Franklin-Williams Museum, N.Y. Symphonia, Center for Deaf Children (Chicago). Mem. American Journalism Alliance, Princeton C. (N.Y.C.). Office: March Building, 12 Codington Pl New York City NY 10008

EARLES, ELEANOR (MRS. OLIVER HENRY), journalist; b. Cadmus, Fla., Nov. 8, 1931; d. Joseph and Alma Wayne Molinaro; B.A. Barnard, 1952; m. Oliver Henry Earles, 1958 (d. 1959).

Researcher, Life, 1952–54; reporter, N.Y. Post, 1954–58; with Nat'l. Radio, 1958–61, Eleanor Earles Interviews; Nat'l. Television Net.: Eleanor Earles Interviews, 1961–65; with U.B.C., 1965– ; Midday Dateline Washington, 1965–67; Gen. Ass'n. Evening News, 1967–74; Eleanor Earles Interviews, 1974–. Author: Eleanor Earles Interviews, 1966. Recipient Philpot Award, 1961. Dir. O.H.E. Interests, Inc., 1959–. Mem. American Journalism Alliance, Together (Wash., D.C.). Office: U.B.C., U.N. Plz New York City NY 10017

Fletch put *Who's Who* back on the shelf and crossed the lobby to the post office, where he bought a large, insulated envelope.

Then he went to Room 82 to borrow the cassette tape recorder from the newly laconic Robert McConnell.

Much of the remainder of the morning he spent in his room, splicing tape.

Finished, he placed all the reels of used tape in the envelope (except the one spliced reel he left ready to play in his marvelous machine) and addressed the envelope to Alston Chambers, an attorney he knew in California. Boldly, he marked the envelope: "HOLD FOR I. M. FLETCHER."

On the way to lunch, Fletch returned McConnell's tape recorder and mailed the envelope.

Thirty-two

Main Dining Room

Captain Andrew Neale was at the luncheon table for six, with Crystal Faoni and, of course, Fredericka Arbuthnot. No Robert McConnell. No Lewis Graham. No Eleanor Earles.

"Has anyone noticed," Fletch asked, "that anyone who shares a meal with the three of us never returns?"

"It's because you get along so well with everybody," Freddie said.

"Whom shall we have for lunch today?" Crystal asked. "Poor Captain Neale. Our next victim."

Sitting straight in his light, neat jacket, Captain Neale smiled distantly at what was clearly an in-joke.

"You're not thinking of keeping us all here beyond tomorrow morning, are you?" Crystal asked.

"Tonight, you mean," said Freddie. "I have to leave on the six-forty-five flight."

"You're not keeping us beyond the end of the convention." Crystal was only passably interested in her fruit salad.

"I don't see how I can," Captain Neale said. "Almost everyone here has made a point of telling me how important he or she is. Such a lot of important people. The seas would rumble and nations would crumble if

210

I kept any of you out of circulation for many more minutes than I had to."

Crystal said to Fletch, "I told you I'd like this guy."

"Have people been beastly to you?" Freddie, grinning, asked Neale.

"I thought reporters were people who report the news," Neale said. "The last couple of days, I've gotten the impression they are the news."

"Right," Crystal said solemnly to her fruit salad. "News does not happen unless a reporter is there to report it."

"For example," said Fletch, "if no one had known World War Two was happening. . . ."

"Actually," Crystal said, "Hitler without the use of the radio wouldn't have been Hitler at all."

"And the Civil War," said Freddie. "If it hadn't been for the telegraph. . . ."

"The geographic center of the American Revolution," Fletch said, "was identical to the center of the new American printing industry."

"And then there was Caesar," Crystal said. "Was he a military genius with pen in hand, or a literary genius with sword in hand? Did Rome conquer the world in reality, or just its communications systems?"

"Weighty matters we discuss at these conventions," Freddie said.

"Listen," Crystal said. "You know I take such comments personally. If I had two breakfasts, blame Fletch. Did you try those blueberry muffins this morning?"

"I tried only one of them," Freddie said.

Crystal said, "The rest of them were good, too."

Captain Neale was chuckling at their foolishness.

Fletch said to him, "People here have given you a pretty rough time, uh?"

Captain Neale stared at his plate a moment before answering.

"It's been like trying to sing 'Strawberry Fields Forever' while your head's stuck in a beehive."

"Literary fella," Crystal told her salad.

"Musical, too," said Freddie.

"Questioning them, they question me."

"Reporters ain't got no humility," Crystal said.

"When they do answer a question," Neale continued, "they know exactly how to answer it—for their own sakes. They know exactly how to present facts absolutely to their own benefit—what to reveal, and what to conceal."

"I suppose so," said Freddie. "Never thought of it that way."

"I'd rather be questioning the full bench of the Supreme Court."

"There are only nine of them," said Freddie.

Crystal said, "I'd say from reading the press you've given away very little. There have been no newsbreaks—except for Poynton's—since the beginning."

"Poynton's?" Neale asked.

"Stuart Poynton. You didn't read him this morning?"

"No," Neale said. "I didn't."

"He said you want to question a man named Joseph Molinaro regarding the murder of Walter March."

"That was in the newspaper?" asked Neale.

"Who is Joseph Molinaro?" Crystal asked.

Neale smiled. "I suppose you'd like to know."

"Oh, no," Crystal said airily. "I've just been through a list of those attending the convention, a list of all hotel employees, the voting list in the town of Hendricks, the membership list of the American Journalism Alliance, Who's Who, and, by telephone, the morgue of People magazine. . . ."

"You must be curious," commented Neale.

Freddie said, "Who is Joseph Molinaro?"

Captain Neale said, "This is the perfect day for a fruit salad. Don't you think?"

"In a way," Fletch said, quietly, "everyone here is a bastard of Walter March. Or has been treated like one."

Neale dropped his fork, but caught it before it went into his lap.

Crystal said brightly, as if introducing a new topic, "Say, who is this Joseph Molinaro, anyway?"

Neale, applying himself to his lunch, seemingly unperturbed, said, "There is no way I can keep any of you beyond tomorrow morning, or tonight, or whenever."

"I understand I'm on the six-forty-five flight out of here." Fletch looked at Freddie. "Me and my shadow. I'm catching a nine o'clock from Washington to London."

She did not look at him.

Fletch said to Neale, "I don't see how you could have accomplished very much, in just a couple of days. Under the circumstances."

"We've accomplished more than you think," Neale said.

"What have you accomplished?" Crystal asked like a sledgehammer.

To Neale's silence, Fletch said, "Captain Neale has narrowed it down to two or three people. Or he wouldn't be letting the rest of us go."

Neale was paying more attention to the remainder of his salad than Crystal would do after trekking across a full golf course.

Fletch hitched himself forward in the chair and addressed himself to Crystal, speaking slowly. "The key," he said, "is that Walter March was murdered—stabbed in the back with a pair of scissors—shortly before eight o'clock Monday morning, in the sitting room of his suite."

213

Crystal stared at him dumbly.

"People lose sight of the simplicities," Fletch said.

Under the table, Freddie kicked him hard, on the shin.

Fletch said, "Ow."

"I just felt like doing that," she said.

"Damnit." He rubbed his shin. "Are you trying to tell me I don't get along well with everybody?"

"Something like that."

"Well, you're wrong," Fletch said. "I do."

The waiter was bringing chocolate cake for dessert.

"Oh, yum!" said Crystal. "Who cares about death and perdition as long as there's chocolate cake?"

"Captain Neale does," said Fletch.

"No," said Neale. "I care about chocolate cake."

"There is evidence," Fletch said, the pain in his shin having abated, "that Walter March was expecting someone—someone he knew. He was expecting someone to call upon him in his suite at eight o'clock or shortly before." Fletch had a forkful of the cake. "Someone to whom he would have opened the door."

Freddie was continuing to look disgusted, but she was listening carefully.

Neale appeared to be paying no attention whatsoever.

Fletch asked him, mildly, "Who was it?"

"Good cake," Neale said.

Fletch said, "Was it Oscar Perlman?"

Neale didn't need to answer.

He looked at Fletch, both alarm and despair in his eyes.

"And who was it who told you Walter March was expecting Oscar Perlman?" Fletch asked. "Junior?"

Neale's throat was dry from the cake. "Junior?"

"Walter March, Junior," Fletch said.

"Jesus!" Neale's eyes went from one to the other

214

of them, desperately. "Don't you print this. None of you. I didn't say a word. If one of you prints. . . ."

"Don't worry." Fletch put his napkin on the table, and stood up. "Crystal and I are unemployed. And Freddie Arbuthnot," he said, "doesn't work for *Newsworld* magazine."

Thirty-three

1:30 P.M.

MY EIGHT TERMS IN THE WHITE HOUSE
Address by Leona Hatch
Main Dining Room

Fletch said, "Mrs. March, I've been trying to understand why you murdered your husband."

Sitting in a chair across the coffee table from him in Suite 12, her expression changed little. Perhaps her eyes grew a little wider.

"And," Fletch said, "I think I do understand."

He had appeared at her door, carrying the marvelous machine.

She had answered the door, still dressed in black, having returned from the memorial service shortly before. Near the door was a luncheon tray waiting to be taken away.

At first, she looked at him in surprise, as it was an unseemly time to call. Then she obviously remembered he had promised they would talk again about his working for March Newspapers. And the suitcase in his hand suggested he was about to leave.

He said nothing.

Sitting on the divan, he placed the marvelous machine flat on the coffee table.

Now he was opening it.

"Statistically, of course," he said, "in the case of a

216

domestic murder—and this is a domestic murder—when a husband or wife is murdered, chances of the spouse being the murderer are something over seventy percent."

Perhaps her eyes widened again when she saw that what was in the suitcase was a tape recorder.

"Which is why," Fletch said, "you chose to murder your husband here at the convention, where you knew your husband would be surrounded by people who had reason to hate him to the point of murder."

Her back was straight. Her hands were folded in her lap.

"Listen to this."

Fletch started the tape recorder.

It was the tape of Lydia March being questioned by Captain Neale, edited:

"At what time did you wake up, Mrs. March?"

"I'm not sure. Seven-fifteen? Seven-twenty? I heard the door to the suite close."

"That was me, Mister Neale," Junior said. "I went down to the lobby to get the newspapers."

"Walter had left his bed. It's always been a thing with him to be up a little earlier than I. A masculine thing. I heard him moving around the bathroom. I lay in bed a little while, a few minutes, really, waiting for him to be done."

"The bathroom door was closed?"

"Yes. In a moment I heard the television here in the living room go on, softly—one of those morning news and features network shows Walter always hated so much—so I got up and went into the bathroom."

"Excuse me. How did your husband get from the bathroom to the living room without coming back through your bedroom?"

"He went through Junior's bedroom, of course. He didn't want to disturb me. . . ."

"... Okay. You were in the bathroom. The television was playing softly in the living room. ..."

"I heard the door to the suite close again, so I thought Walter had gone down for coffee."

"Had the television gone off?"

"No."

"So, actually, someone could have come into the suite at that point."

"No. At first, I thought Junior might have come back, but he couldn't have."

"Why not?"

"I didn't hear them talking."

"Would they have been talking? Necessarily?"

"Of course. ..."

"So, Mrs. March, you think you heard the suite door close again, but your husband hadn't left the suite, and you think no one entered the suite because you didn't hear talking?"

"I guess that's right. I could be mistaken, of course. I'm trying to reconstruct."

"Pardon, but where were you physically in the bathroom when you heard the door close the second time?"

"I was getting into the tub. ..."

"... You had already run the tub?"

"Yes. While I was brushing my teeth. And all that."

"So there must have been a period of time, while the tub was running, that you couldn't have heard anything from the living room—not the front door, not the television, not talking?"

"I suppose not."

"So the second time you heard the door close, when you were getting into the tub, you actually could have been hearing someone leave the suite."

"Oh, my. That's right. Of course."

"It would explain your son's not having returned,

your husband's not having left, and your not hearing talking."

"How clever you are. . . ."

Fletch switched off the marvelous machine.

Listening, Lydia March's eyes had gone back and forth from the slowly revolving tape reel to Fletch's face.

Fletch said, "When I first arrived at Hendricks Plantation, and Helena Williams was telling me about the murder, I noticed she particularly mentioned what you had heard from the bathroom. I think she said something about your hearing gurgling and thinking it was the tub drain. Not precisely what you said here. But Helena could have reported what you heard from the bathroom only if you had made a point of telling her."

Fletch rested his back against a divan pillow.

"Captain Neale wasn't a bit clever," he said. "He never went into the bathroom to discover what could be heard from there.

"I did."

"Last night, when I came to visit you, you and Jake Williams were talking here in the living room. I went into the bathroom. The doors of both bedrooms to the living room were open—which gave me a much better chance to hear than you supposedly had. I closed both bathroom doors. I did not run water. I did not flush the toilet. I listened.

"Mrs. March, I could not hear you and Jake talking. You could not have heard the television, especially on low.

"I did not hear Jake leave the suite. You could not have heard the door closing—as you said you did.

"Perhaps your hearing is better than mine, but my hearing is forty years younger than yours.

"As Oscar Perlman might say, I have twenty-twenty hearing.

"Mrs. March, the closets to both bedrooms are between the bathroom and the living room. Architects do this on purpose, so you cannot hear.

"You made too much of an issue of the front door of the suite being open. You gave evidence you couldn't have had. It was important for you to convince everyone that you heard the door close when Junior left the suite, but that it was open when you came into the living room.

"You lied.

"Why?

"Despite everything we know about your husband, how badly he treated people, his private detectives, his sense of security, you had to convince people he had opened the door to someone else, who stabbed him in the back.

"Simplicity. The simple truth is that there were two of you in a suite, with the door to the corridor closed and locked, and one of you was stabbed.

"Who did it?"

He leaned forward again, and again pressed the PLAY button on the tape recorder.

Lydia March's voice came from the speakers:

". . . There was a man in the corridor, walking away, lighting a cigar as he walked . . . I didn't know who he was, from behind . . . I ran toward him . . . then I realized who he was. . . ."

"Mrs. March. Who was the man in the corridor?"

"Perlman. Oscar Perlman."

"The humorist?"

"If you say so. . . ."

Fletch switched off the machine again.

He said, "Mrs. March, you made three mistakes in laying down potential evidence that Oscar Perlman is your husband's murderer.

"The first isn't very serious. Perlman says he was

playing poker until five-thirty in the morning and then slept late. That he was playing poker until five-thirty in the morning can be confirmed, and I suppose Neale has done so. He could have gotten up, murdered your husband, and gone back to bed, or whatever, but it doesn't seem likely.

"A much more serious mistake you made is in the timing of it all.

"According to your story, someone stabbed your husband in the living room. Sitting in the bathtub, you heard choking, whatever, called out, got out of the tub, grabbed a towel, went into the bedroom, saw your husband stagger in from the living room, roll off the bed, drive the scissors deeper into his back, arch up, et cetera, and die. Then you ran through the bedroom, the living room, and into the corridor.

"And you try to indicate that the man who might have stabbed your husband is—just at that point—still in the corridor, walking away?

"You lied.

"Why?

"The third mistake you made in saying Oscar Perlman was in the corridor outside the suite is most serious.

"But I'll come back to that."

Again, Fletch settled himself on the divan.

He said, "Unfortunately for you, the people who had the best motives and opportunity to kill your husband are all highly skilled at handling an interview. They're all reporters. Rolly Wisham, for example, did nothing to divert suspicion from himself. Oscar Perlman didn't even pretend he had an alibi. Lewis Graham didn't hesitate to be open—almost indict himself. Even Crystal Faoni was quick to realize she was a possible suspect—and didn't hesitate to admit it. Perhaps it was unconscious on their parts, but I think they all have

221

enough experience to have realized instinctively they had all been set up as clay pigeons.

"By you. By your choice of the time and the place of the murder.

"I always look for the controlling intelligence behind anything and everything. In this case, it was yours.

"Why? Why, why, why?"

Lydia March continued sitting primly in her chair. Her head had raised slightly, and she was looking somewhat down her nose at him.

"In October, 1928, you married Walter March, who was due to graduate from Princeton in June, 1929.

"Odd. Especially in those days. Not to have waited for graduation.

"Not so odd. Junior was born five months later, in March, 1929.

"What was the expression for it in those days? A shotgun marriage?

"Was Walter March the father of your child?

"Or, being the heir to a newspaper fortune, was he just the best catch around?

"Were you sure Walter was the father? Was he?

"You're a wily woman, Mrs. March.

"You remained married to Walter March for fifty years. Never had another child.

"There was an enormous newspaper fortune to be inherited.

"But Walter was an old war-horse. He wouldn't give up. Perfect health. He announced his retirement once, and then, when Junior goofed up, didn't retire.

"And all this time, as Junior was getting to be fifty years old, losing his wife, his family, drinking more and more, you saw him becoming weaker and weaker, wasting away."

Fletch stared a long moment at the floor.

Finally, he said, "There is a time for fathers to move

aside, to quit, to die, to leave room for their sons to grow.

"Even if they are just the image of the father, rather than the blood-father.

"Walter wasn't moving aside.

"Did he somehow know, instinctively, Walter, Junior, wasn't his son?"

Fletch jerked the marvelous machine's wire from the wall socket.

"You killed your husband to save your son."

He was wrapping up the wire. "Do you know your husband had another son? His name is Joseph Molinaro. Your husband had him with Eleanor Earles, I guess, while she was a student at Barnard.

"And did you know that Joseph Molinaro is here?

"He came here to see your husband.

"Maybe another son on the horizon—if you knew it—made you even more desperate to protect your own son."

Fletch closed and latched the cover of the suitcase.

"Of course, I'm going to have to talk with Captain Neale—if you don't first.

"By the way," he said. "Thanks for the job offer.

"Same way you Marches do everything. Either buy people off, or blackmail them into a corner.

"After more than a century of this, you have a most uncanny instinct as to whom to buy off or blackmail."

He stood up and picked up the suitcase.

"Oh," he said. "The third, most terrible mistake you made in saying Oscar Perlman was in the corridor was that you said it in Junior's presence.

"The big idiot has blown the game again.

"He's gone and told Captain Neale that Perlman had an appointment to see your husband at eight o'clock Monday morning."

Lydia was looking up at Fletch from her chair.

Her expression did not change at all.

Fletch said, "You don't understand the significance of that, do you?"

Her expression still didn't change.

"Again, Junior was overdoing the clever bit. Why would he lie to support you, unless he knows you were lying?

"He knows you killed your husband."

Her eyes lowered, slowly.

Her lips tightened, and turned down at their corners.

Her eyes settled on her hands, in her lap.

Slowly, her hands opened, and turned palms up.

"Mrs. March," Fletch said. "You're killing your son."

Fletch was almost back to his room, carrying the marvelous machine, before he realized that during the time he had just spent with her, Lydia March had not said one word.

Thirty-four

3:00 P.M.
ARRIVAL OF THE PRESIDENT OF THE UNITED STATES
(Cancelled)
ARRIVAL OF THE VICE-PRESIDENT OF THE UNITED STATES

Fletch heard the helicopter banging away overhead as he crossed the lobby to the French doors.

Most of the conventioneers were on the terrace behind Hendricks Plantation House to watch the helicopter land on the lawn. The sunlight brought out the bright colors of their clothes. Mostly they were still chattering about Leona Hatch's insider's report on her eight terms as a White House reporter.

When Fletch came onto the terrace, the helicopter had retreated to the sky over the far ridge of trees.

Leona Hatch pulled herself away from an admiring group of young people, and approached Fletch.

"I'll swear I know you," she said. "With my dying breath, I'll swear."

He put her hand out to her.

"Fletcher," he said. "Irwin Fletcher."

She shook hands, limply, her eyes searching his face, sharply.

"I feel I know you very well," she said.

Fletch was looking for Captain Neale.

Junior, sallow and slump-shouldered, was standing with Jake Williams, watching the helicopter.

225

"I can't get over this feeling, this certainty, that I know you well," Leona Hatch said. "But I can't remember. . . ."

Fletch saw Neale standing with some uniformed Virginia State policemen.

"Excuse me," he said to Leona Hatch.

He touched Neale's elbow.

Neale looked at him.

The slight expression of annoyance in Neale's face was replaced by a gentle, respectful curiosity.

Obviously, Neale was remembering from lunch that Fletch seemed to know more about the murder of Walter March than the others did, and, in addition, could make some very good guesses.

Fletch said, quietly, "I think you should go talk with Lydia March."

Neale looked at Fletch a moment, probably considering questions to ask, but deciding not to ask any.

Captain Neale nodded, and went through the crowd and into the lobby of the hotel.

The helicopter was approaching the lawn below the terrace very slowly.

Fletch had been aware that a group of five men, moving together, had come onto the terrace.

It was not until they were standing at the front of the terrace, next to Junior and Jake Williams, that Fletch looked directly at the men.

Hands in pockets, appearing totally relaxed, watching the helicopter land, was the Vice-President of the United States.

Helena Williams spotted him the same time Fletch did.

She began to rush toward him from the other side of the terrace.

What she was saying was drowned out by the noise of the helicopter.

Junior, remaining oblivious to the presence of the Vice-President of the United States beside him, suddenly rocked back on his heels.

He put his hand up to his face, as if he were about to sneeze.

Fletch saw blood on Junior's neck.

Then a splotch of blood appeared on Junior's white shirt, next to his necktie.

Fletch started toward Junior.

Junior lost his balance and fell against the Vice-President.

Someone screamed.

Jake Williams yelled, "Junior!"

Junior rolled as he fell.

Landing on his back on the flagstones, the two splotches of blood, on his neck and on his shirt, were clearly visible.

Helena was kneeling over him.

Even over the sound of the helicopter, Fletch could hear Jake Williams shout, "Someone is trying to kill the Vice-President!"

One of the four men with the Vice-President spun him around, toward the hotel.

The other three surrounded him closely.

One held his hand out behind the Vice-President's head, as if to shield him from the sun.

They pushed him through the crowd into the hotel.

Crystal Faoni had joined Helena Williams in kneeling over Junior.

Crystal was trying to blow air into Junior's mouth.

The helicopter had settled on the lawn, and its door was opening.

Fletch looked across the lawn, and ran his eyes as closely as he could along the line of trees.

Men in Marine Corps uniform were getting off the helicopter.

At first, Fletch moved very slowly, backing away from the crowd, turning, jumping off the terrace, ambling across the lawn.

He did not break into a full run for the stables until he was well-concealed by the trees.

Thirty-five

Fletch had no plan.

He could find no one at the stables, so he saddled the horse he had used twice before, fumbling, as he hadn't saddled a horse himself in a long time, alarming the horse with his haste.

Once clear of the paddock area, he laid the whip on her and she poured on speed, but only for a very few moments.

She was a pleasant horse, but not too swift.

Clearly, in all her days on Hendricks Plantation, she had never been asked to be in a sincere hurry.

By the time they had climbed the ridge and were approaching the camper along the timber road she was winded and resentful.

Fletch left her in the deep shade of the woods about twenty meters up the hillside from the camper.

He still had no plan.

The camper was open, but the keys weren't in the ignition.

He looked for the keys under the driver's seat, over the visor, in the map compartment, then, hurrying, moved back into the camper, flipping over the mattress of the unmade bed, glancing in the cabinets, the oven, under the seat cushions of the two chairs.

He went through the pockets of a dark suit hanging from a curtain rod.

On a shelf was an old cigar box. Inside were screws, nails, a few sockets for a wrench, half a pouch of Bull Durham tobacco, and a set of keys, somewhat rusted.

He tried the keys in the ignition.

The third key on the chain fit.

He left it in the ignition.

Standing by the camper, he realized he still didn't have a plan.

From down the road, around the bend, he heard someone cough.

Mentally, Fletch thanked his horse, up in the woods, for being quiet.

Fletch flattened himself against the wall of the camper, next to the rear wheels.

He stuck his head out for a look only once.

Joseph Molinaro was walking toward the camper, ten meters away, a rifle under his right arm.

It had not occurred to Fletch before this that, of course, Joseph Molinaro would be carrying a rifle.

He had not thought to arm himself.

There was no time to go back into the camper.

The few branches and stones in the road at his feet were too small and light to make good weapons.

He had no more time to think.

Fletch had left the camper through the driver's door.

Molinaro was at the back of the camper, heading for the door near the right rear wheels.

Crouching, looking under the camper, Fletch watched Molinaro's feet.

As soon as Molinaro was on the other side of the camper, Fletch moved around to its rear and along its wall.

Just as Molinaro was beginning to climb the three steps into the camper, beginning to bend to go through the door, Fletch hit him on the back of his head, hard, with the side of his hand.

The force of the blow knocked Molinaro's head against the solid door frame.

Instinctively tightening his arm over the rifle, Molinaro fell up the steps, half-in and half-out of the camper.

He rolled over.

His eyes remained open only a second or two.

He appeared to recognize Fletch.

Having already been unconscious once that morning, Molinaro's head settled back on the camper's floor, and he went deeply unconscious.

Fletch took the rifle from under his arm and slid it along the floor of the camper, toward the front.

Picking up Molinaro's legs, Fletch slid his back along the linoleum floor until Molinaro was entirely aboard the camper and the door could be closed.

Fletch climbed the steps to the camper and stepped over Molinaro.

He tore two strips from the bed sheet and tied Molinaro's ankles together.

Then he tied his wrists together, in front of him.

He slammed the back door of the camper, climbed into the driver's seat, and turned the key in the ignition.

The battery was dead.

Incredulous, Fletch senselessly tried the key three or four times.

He groaned.

Molinaro couldn't do anything right.

He had come to Virginia to meet his father.

Never did meet him.

That morning he had gotten up, flicked a cigarette into a stranger's face, and instantly was knocked unconscious.

Then he had let two people know who he was and why he was there.

If the suit hanging from the curtain rod was any indication, Joseph Molinaro actually had gone to Walter March's Memorial Service.

Next, using that rifle on the floor with telescopic sights, he had murdered his half brother.

He had ambled back to his camper, not even having thrown the murder weapon away, never thinking someone who had figured out what he had done might be waiting for him.

And the battery of his getaway vehicle was dead.

Looking at the man, with the tight, curly gray hair, dressed in the blue jeans jacket, unconscious and bound on the floor of the camper, Fletch shook his head.

Then he climbed the hillside and got his horse.

"I see you figured it out just a little faster than I did."

Before leaving the timber road, Fletch met Frank Gillis heading for the camper.

Gillis' horse looked exhausted.

Gillis nodded at Molinaro slung over the saddle of Fletch's horse.

"Is he dead, or just unconscious?"

"Unconscious."

Gillis said, "He seems to spend a lot of time in that condition."

"Poor son of a bitch."

Walking the horse, Fletch held the reins in his right hand, the rifle in his left.

He asked, "Junior dead?"

"Yeah."

Fletch left the road and started through the woods, down the hillside.

Gillis said, "You sure that's the murder weapon?"

"As sure as I can be, without a ballistics test. It's

the weapon he was carrying when he returned to the camper."

Remaining on his horse, Gillis followed Fletch through the woods to the pasture and then rode along beside him.

Fletch said, "I wonder if you'd mind putting Molinaro on your horse?"

"Why?"

"I feel silly. I feel like I'm walking into Dodge City."

"So why should I feel silly?"

Frank Gillis chuckled.

"One of us has to feel silly, and you're the one who caught him," Gillis said.

"Thanks."

"Why didn't you use the camper?"

"Dead battery."

Gillis shook his head, just as Fletch had.

"I don't know," Gillis said. "This guy . . . did he murder old man March, or did he think Junior murdered him? Or was he just plain jealous of Junior, now that Molinaro's dream of being recognized by his father was over?"

Fletch walked along quietly a moment, before saying, "You'll have to ask Captain Neale, I guess."

"You know," Gillis said, "everyone thought an attempt was being made on the Vice-President's life."

"Yeah."

"I did, too, at first, until I realized this was another March who was dead. Who'd ever want to kill the Vice-President of the United States? One could have a greater effect upon national policy by killing the White House cook."

"Who was in the helicopter?" Fletch asked.

"Oh, that." Gillis' chins were quivering with mirth. "Some Marine Corps General. He was here for some ceremony or other, a presentation of some kind, pin a medal on someone. And while the General was making this big entrance, landing in a helicopter on the back lawn, the Vice-President of the United States was arriving at the front of the hotel in an economy-size car—completely ignored."

They were both laughing, and Molinaro was still unconscious.

"As soon as everyone realized what had happened, that Junior had been shot, the Secret Service hustled the Vice-President back into his car, and back to Washington, and the General climbed aboard his helicopter and took off. The only thing the Vice-President was heard to say, during his stay at Hendricks Plantation, was, 'My! The military live well!' "

They came onto the back lawns of Hendricks Plantation.

Indeed, the helicopter was gone.

People were playing golf on the rolling greens the other side of the plantation house.

"You want to carry the rifle?" Fletch asked.

"No, no. I wouldn't take from your moment of glory."

Fletch said, "This isn't glory."

Captain Neale saw them from the terrace, and came down to the lawn to meet them.

A couple of uniformed State Policemen followed him.

Neale indicated the man across the saddle of Fletch's horse.

"Who's that?" he asked.

Fletch said, "Joseph Molinaro."

"Can't be," Neale said. "Molinaro's only about thirty. Younger."

Still on his horse, Gillis said, "Look at his face."

Neale lifted Molinaro's head by the hair.

234

"My, my," Neale said.

Fletch handed his reins to one of the uniformed policemen.

Neale asked Fletch, "Did Molinaro kill young March?"

Fletch handed Neale the rifle. "Easy to prove. This is the weapon he was carrying."

Over Neale's shoulder, Fletch saw Eleanor Earles appear on the terrace.

"Did you speak to Lydia March?" Fletch asked Neale.

"No."

"No?"

Neale said, "She's dead. Overdose. Seconal."

Eleanor Earles was approaching them.

Even at a distance, Fletch could see the set of her face. It seemed frozen.

"She left a note," Neale said. "To Junior. Saying she wouldn't say why, but she had murdered her husband. The key thing is, she said the night they arrived she went back downstairs to the reception desk to order flowers for the suite, and stole the scissors she had seen on the desk when they'd checked in. Now that he's reminded of it, the desk clerk says he was puzzled at the time why she hadn't telephoned the order down. He had also been slightly insulted, because flowers had been put in all the suites, and Mrs. March had said the flowers in Suite 3 were simply inadequate."

Eleanor Earles was standing near them, staring at the man slung over the saddle.

Neale noticed her.

"Hey," he said to the uniformed policemen, "let's get this guy off the horse."

Gillis got off his horse, to help.

Eleanor Earles watched them take Molinaro off the horse and put him on the ground.

In a moment, her face still frozen, she turned and walked back toward the hotel.

From what Fletch had seen, there was no way Eleanor Earles could have known, from that distance, whether her son was dead or alive.

Thirty-six

"Good afternoon. The *Boston Star*."

"Jack Saunders, please."

Fletch had gone directly to Room 102—Crystal Faoni's room—and banged on the door.

Tired and teary, she opened the door.

Fletch guessed that, badly upset by her experience of trying to breathe life into a dead man—into a dead Walter March, Junior—Crystal had been napping fully clad on her bed in the dark room.

"Wake up," Fletch said. "Cheer up."

"Really, Fletch, at this moment I'm not sure I can stand your relentless cheer."

He entered her room while she still held onto the doorknob.

He pulled the drapes open.

"Close the door," he said.

She sighed. And closed the door.

"What's the best way to get a job in the newspaper business?" he asked.

She thought a moment. "I suppose have a story no one else has. A real scoop. Is this another game?"

"I've got a story for you," he said. "A real scoop. And, maybe, if we work it right, a job in Boston with Jack Saunders."

"A job for me?"

"Yes. Sit down while I explain."

237

"Fletch, I don't need a story from you. I can get my own story. Amusing lad though you are, I sort of resent the idea I need to get a story from you or from anyone else."

"You're talking like a woman."

"You noticed."

"Why are you talking like a woman?"

"Because you're talking like a man? You come bounding in here, offering to give me a story, arrange a job for me, as if I were someone who has to be taken care of, as if you, The Big He, are the source of The Power and The Glory Forever and Ever. Ah, men!"

"Golly, you speak well," Fletch said. "You just make that up?"

"Just occasionally, Fletch, you have problems with male chauvinism. I've mentioned it to you."

"Yes, you have."

"I know you try hard to correct yourself and better yourself but, Fletcher, darling, remember there can be no end to the self-improvement bit."

"Thank you. Now may we get on to the matter at hand?"

"No."

"No?"

"No. I'm not accepting a story from you. I'm not accepting a job from you. I wouldn't even accept dinner from you."

"What?"

"Well. Maybe I'd accept dinner."

After his ride into the hills to find Joseph Molinaro and his long walk back, Fletch was feeling distinctly chilled by Crystal's air conditioner.

"Crystal, do you think this is the way Bob McConnell would respond to such an offer from me?"

"No."

"Stuart Poynton?"

"Of course not."

"Tim Shields?"

"They're not women."

"They're also not friends."

He popped his eyes at her.

She looked away.

Neither of them had sat down.

He said, "Do you mind if I turn down your air-conditioning?"

"Go ahead."

"Can a man and woman be friends?" he asked.

He found the air conditioner controls. They had been set to HIGH. He turned them to LOW.

"Are friends people who consider each other?" he asked.

She said, "I can get my own story."

"Do you know Lydia March killed herself?" he asked.

"No."

"Do you know she killed her husband?"

"No."

"Do you know that the shooting this afternoon was not an unsuccessful attempt on the life of the Vice-President, but a successful attempt on the life of Walter March, Junior?"

"No."

"Do you know who killed Walter March, Junior?"

"No. But I can find out. Why are you telling me all this?"

"You can't find out in time to scoop everyone else and get a job with Jack Saunders on the Boston *Star*."

"If you know all this, why don't you use it? You haven't got a job either."

"I'm working on a book, Crystal. In Italy. On Edgar Arthur Tharp, Junior."

"Oh, yeah." She fiddled around the room, continuing to look unwell. "You don't have to give me anything."

"Crystal, I have to get on a plane in a couple of hours. I can't afford to miss it. I can't do the follow-ups on this story. Now will you sit down?"

"Is all this true?" she asked. "What you just said? Did Lydia March kill herself?"

"Cross my heart and hope to die in a cellarful of Walter March's private detectives. Will you listen, please?"

She sat in a light chair.

At first, clearly, part of her mind was still on the terrace, kneeling over Walter March's son, trying to breathe life into him; clearly, another part of her mind was still wondering why Fletch was insisting on giving her the biggest story of the year, of her career. . . .

"You're not listening," Fletch said. "Please. You've got to be able to phone this story in pretty soon."

Gradually, as her attention focused on what he was saying, her eyes widened, color came back to her cheeks, her back straightened.

Then she began saying, "Fletch, you can't know this."

"I'm giving you much more background than you need, just so you'll believe me."

"But there is no way you could know all this. It's not humanly possible."

"Not all my methods are human," he said.

And she would say, "Fletch, are you sure?"

And she would repeat, "Fletch, how do you know all this?"

"I have a marvelous machine."

Finally, as the pieces fitted together, she became convinced.

"Hell of a story!" she said.

Despite her initial resistance and inattention, Fletch

240

saw there was no reason to repeat any part of the story to Crystal.

She said, "Wow!"

Fletch picked up the telephone and put the call through.

"Who's calling?" a grumpy male voice finally asked.

"I. M. Fletcher."

"Who?"

"Just tell Jack Saunders a guy named Fletcher wants to talk to him."

Immediately, Jack Saunders' voice came on the line.

"I was hoping you'd call," he said.

"How do, Jack. Remember telling me you'd give a job to anyone who scooped the Walter March story?"

"Did I say that?"

"You did."

"Fletch, I said. . . ."

"Remember Crystal Faoni? She used to work with us in Chicago."

"I remember she's even fatter than my wife. Hell of a lot brighter, though."

"Jack, she has the story."

"What story?"

"The Walter March story. The whole thing. Tied in a neat, big bundle."

"Last time we talked, you listed her as a suspect in the Walter March murder."

"I just wanted to bring up her name. Jog your memory. Let you know she's here, at the convention."

"Crystal has the Walter March story?"

"Crystal has the job?"

There was only the slightest hesitation.

"Crystal has the job."

Fletch said, "Crystal has the Walter March story."

"Let me talk to her a minute," Jack Saunders said, "before I ask her to dictate into the recorder."

"Sure, Jack, sure."

Crystal came to the phone.

"Hello, Jack? How's Daphne?"

Crystal listened a moment while doubtlessly Jack Saunders said something imaginative and rotten about his wife and she laughed and shook her head at Fletch.

"Say, Jack? You'd better slip me on the payroll pretty quick. My savings are about gone. This has been an expensive convention. Too much to eat around here."

Fletch put the air conditioner dial back on MEDIUM.

Crystal would be on the phone a long time, and it would be hot work.

"Sure, Jack," Crystal said. "I'm ready to dictate. Switch me over to the recorder. I'll see you in Boston Monday."

Fletch opened the door.

"Oh, boy!" Crystal, waiting for the *Star* to straighten out its electronics, cupped her hand over the telephone receiver. "Scoopin' Freddie."

Absently, Fletch said, "What?"

"Scoopin' this story will put me right up there in the big league with Freddie Arbuthnot."

"Who?"

"Freddie Arbuthnot," Crystal said conversationally. "Don't you read her stuff? She's terrific."

"What?"

"Didn't you read her on the Pecuchet trial? In Arizona? Real award-winning stuff. She's the greatest. Oh, yeah. You were in Italy."

"You mean, Freddie. . . ."

Crystal, round-eyed, looked at him from the telephone.

Fletch said, "You mean, Freddie is. . . ."

"What's the matter, Fletch?"

"You mean, Freddie Arbuthnot is. . . ."

"What?"

242

"You mean, Freddie Arbuthnot is . . . Freddie Arbuthnot?"

"Who did you think she is," Crystal asked, "Paul McCartney?"

"Oh, my God." Verily, Fletch did smite his forehead. "I never looked her up!"

As he began to stagger through the door, Crystal said, "Hey, Fletch."

He looked at her dumbly.

Crystal said, "Thanks. Friend."

Thirty-seven

"Nice of you to drop by."

Having spent a moment banging on Freddie Arbuthnot's door, Fletch scarcely noticed the door to his own room was open.

Freddie must have left for the airport.

Robert Englehardt and Don Gibbs were in Fletch's room.

Gibbs was looking into Fletch's closet.

Englehardt had opened the marvelous machine on the luggage rack and was examining it.

"I don't have much time to visit," Fletch said. "Got to pack and get to the airport."

"Pretty classy machine," Englehardt said. "Did you use it well?"

"All depends on what you mean by 'well.' "

"Where are the tapes?"

"Oh, they're gone."

Englehardt turned to him.

"Gone?"

"Don, as long as you're in the closet, will you drag my suitcases out?"

"Gone?" Englehardt said.

"Yeah. Gonezo."

Fletch took the two suitcases from Gibbs and opened them on the bed.

"Hand me that suit from the closet, will you, Don?"

Englehardt said, "Mister Fletcher, you're suffering from a misapprehension."

"I'm sure it's nothing aspirin and a good night's sleep can't fix. What about those slacks, Don. Thanks."

"Those men. In Italy. Fabens and Eggers. . . ."

"Eggers, Gordon and Fabens, Richard," helped Fletch.

"They aren't ours."

"No?"

"No."

Through his horn-rimmed glasses, Englehardt's eyes were as solemn as a hoot owl's.

Fletch said, "Gee. Not ours."

"They are not members of the Central Intelligence Agency. They don't work for any American agency. They are not citizens of the United States."

"Anything in that laundry bag, Don?"

"Mister Fletcher, you're not listening."

"Eggers, Gordon and Fabens, Richard are baddies," said Fletch. "I'll bet they're from the other side of the Steel Shade."

Englehardt said, "Which is why Mister Gibbs and I came down here to Hendricks. Foreign agents had set you up to provide them with information to blackmail the American press."

Fletch said, "Gee."

Englehardt said, "I don't see how you could think the Central Intelligence Agency could ever be involved in such an operation."

"I checked," said Fletch. "I asked you."

"We never said we were involved," Englehardt said. "I said you had better go along with the operation. And then Gibbs and I came down here to figure it out."

"And did you figure it out?" Fletch asked.

"We've been working very hard," Englehardt said.

Fletch said, "Yeah."

He took off his shirt and stuffed it into the laundry bag.

After riding and walking around the countryside he needed a shower, but he didn't have time.

Englehardt was saying, "I don't see how anyone could think the C.I.A. would be involved in such an operation. . . ."

In the bathroom, Fletch sprayed himself with underarm deodorant.

Don Gibbs said, "Fletch, did you know those guys weren't from the C.I.A.?"

"I had an inkling."

"You did?"

"I inkled."

"How?"

"Fabens' cigar. It really stank. Had to be Rumanian, Albanian, Bulgarian. Phew! It stank. I mentioned it to him. American clothes. American accent. People get really stuck with their smoking habits." Fletch lifted clean shirts from the bureau drawer to his suitcase. "Then, when the Internal Revenue Service wallah paid me a visit, I figured there were either crossed wires, or no wires at all. There was no good reason for putting that kind of pressure on me at that moment."

He was putting on a clean shirt.

Sternly, Englehardt said, "If you knew—or suspected—Eggers and Fabens weren't from the C.I.A., then why did you give them the tapes?"

"Oh, I didn't," Fletch said.

"You said they're gone."

"The tapes? They are gone."

"You didn't give them to Eggers and Fabens?" Gibbs asked.

"You think I'm crazy?"

"Fletcher," Englehardt said, "we want Eggers and Fabens, and we want those tapes."

"Eggers and Fabens you can have." Fletch took their telegram from the drawer of his bedside table and handed it to Englehardt. "Says here you can pick 'em up tonight at the BOAC counter in Washington, any time between seven-thirty and nine. Very convenient for you."

Fletch grabbed a necktie he had already put in one suitcase. "Also indicates, if you read carefully, that I have not given them the tapes."

Englehardt was holding the telegram, but looking at Fletch.

"Fletcher, where are the tapes?"

"I mailed them. Yesterday."

"To yourself?"

"No."

"To whom did you mail them?"

Fletch checked his suitcases. He had already thrown in his shaving gear.

"I guess that's everything," he said.

"Fletcher," Englehardt said, "you're going to give us those tapes."

"I thought you said the C.I.A. wouldn't be involved in a thing like this."

"As long as the tapes exist. . . . ," Gibbs said.

"The tapes are evidence of information gathered by a foreign power," Englehardt announced.

"Bushwa," said Fletch.

He closed his suitcases.

"Fletcher, do I have to remind you how you were forced to do this job in the first place? Exporting money illegally from the United States? Not being able to state the source of that money? Not filing federal tax returns?"

"Are you blackmailing me?"

"It will be my duty," Englehardt said, "to turn this information over to the proper domestic authorities."

"You know," Gibbs giggled, "we didn't know any of that about you—until you told us."

"You're blackmailing me," Fletch said.

Gibbs was standing behind him and Englehardt was standing near the door.

"There's a tape on the machine," Fletch said. "Actually, it's a copy of a tape. The original was mailed out with the others."

Englehardt looked at the tape on the machine.

"Press the PLAY button," Fletch said.

Englehardt hesitated a moment, apparently wondering what pressing the PLAY button might do to him, then bravely stepped to the machine and pressed the button.

The volume was loud.

They heard Gibbs' voice:

"Snow, beautiful snow! Who'd ever expect snow in Virginia this time of year? . . . Who'd ever think my dear old department headie, Bobby Englehardt, would travel through the South with snow in his attaché case? Good thing it didn't melt!

". . . Well, I've got a surprise for you, too, dear old department headie. 'What's that?' you ask with one voice. Well! I've got a surprise for you! 'Member those two sweet little things in Billy-Bobby's boo-boo-bar lounge? 'Sweet little things,' you say together. Well, sir, I had the piss-pa-cacity to invite them up! To our glorious journalists' suite. This very night! This very hour! This very minute! In fact, for twenty minutes ago."

(*Englehardt's voice*): "You did?"

(*Gibbs' voice*): "I did. Where the hell are they? Got to live like journalists, right? Wild, wild, wicked women. Live it up!"

(*Englehardt's voice*): "I invited someone, too."

(*Gibbs' voice*): "You did? We gonna have four

broads? Four naked, writhing girls? All in the same room?"

(*Englehardt's voice*): "The lifeguard."

Englehardt turned off the marvelous machine.

"The tape continues," Fletch said. "All through what I'm sure your superiors will provincially refer to as your drunken sex orgy. Lots more references to cocaine. Et cetera. 'Switch!' " he quoted Gibbs, but with a drawl. " 'Switch!' "

Englehardt's shoulders had lowered, like those of a bull about to charge.

His fists were clenched.

The skin around his eyes was a dark red.

" 'Live like journalists,' " Fletch quoted. " 'Disgusting.' "

Gibbs was assimilating more slowly. Or he was in a complete state of shock.

His face had gone perfectly white, his jaw slack. Standing, he was staring at the floor about two meters in front of him.

"Of course, this isn't the original tape," Fletch said. "But the original isn't much better. Same cast of characters, same dialogue. . . ."

Gibbs said, "You bugged our room! Goddamn it, Fletcher, you bugged our room!"

"Of course. You think I'm stupid?"

Englehardt's shoulders had slumped somewhat, his fists loosened.

"What are you going to do?" he asked.

"Blackmail you," Fletch answered. "Of course."

He picked up his two suitcases.

"Six weeks from today, I want to receive official, formal notification that all charges against me have been dropped," Fletch said. "Into the Potomac. If not, the careers of Robert Englehardt and Donald Gibbs will be over."

"We can't do that," said Englehardt.

"That's Abuse of Agency!" said Gibbs.

Fletch said, "You'll find a way."

The airport limousine had gone, so Fletch had had to send for a taxi.

He was waiting in front of the hotel with his suitcases.

Don Gibbs came through the glass door of the hotel, toward him, still looking extremely white.

"Fletcher." His voice was low.

"Yeah?"

The taxi was arriving.

"If you had any suspicion at all Eggers and Fabens weren't from the C.I.A., why did you go through with this job?"

"Three reasons."

Fletch handed his suitcases to the driver.

"First, I'm nosy."

Fletch opened the door to the backseat.

"Second, I thought there might be a story in it."

He got into the car.

"Third," Fletch said, just before closing the door, "I didn't want to go to jail."

Thirty-eight

"FREDDIE!"

Her carry-on bag in hand, she was almost at the steps of the twelve-seater airplane.

"FREDDIE!"

His own suitcases banging against his knees, he ran across the airplane parking area.

"FREDDIE!"

Finally, she heard him, and turned to wait for him.

"Listen," he said. Standing before her, he was huffing and puffing.

"Listen," he said. "You're Freddie Arbuthnot."

"No," she said. "I'm Ms. Blake."

"I can explain," he said.

In the late afternoon light, her eyes examined him through narrow slits.

"Uh . . . ," he said.

She waited.

He said, ". . . uh."

And she waited.

"I mean, I can explain," he said. "There is an explanation."

The pilot, in a white short-sleeved shirt and sunglasses, was waiting by the steps for them to board.

"Uh . . . ," Fletch said. "This will take some time."

"We don't have any more time," she said. "Together."

"We do!" he said. "All you have to do is come to Italy with me. Tonight."

"Irwin Fletcher, I have a job to do. I'm employed, you know?"

"A vacation? You could have a nice vacation. Cagna's beautiful this time of year."

"If I had the time, I'd stay here and polish up the Walter March story."

"Polish it up?"

"So far I've only been able to phone in the leaders."

"Leaders? What leaders do you have?"

"Oh, you know. Lydia March's suicide. Her confession note. Junior's murder. Joseph Molinaro. . . ."

"Oh," he said. "Ow."

As if thinking aloud, she said, "I'll have to do the polishing in New York, before Saturday morning."

"Then you could come to Italy," he said. "Saturday."

She said, "You know the Jack Burroughs trial starts Monday."

"Jack Burroughs?"

"Fletcher, you know I won the Mulholland Award for my coverage of the Burroughs case last year."

"Oh, yes," he said. "No, actually, I didn't."

"Fletcher, are you a journalist at all?"

"Off and on," he said. "Off and on."

"I'd think you're a busboy," she said quietly, "except busboys have to get along well with everybody."

Five heads aboard the plane were looking at them through the windows.

"I have to be in Italy," he said. "For about six weeks. Or, I should say, I have to be out of this country for six weeks, more or less."

"Have a nice time."

"Freddie. . . ."

"Irwin. . . ."

"There has to be some way I can explain," he said.

She agreed. "There has to be."

"It's sort of difficult. . . ."

Her eyes were still squinted against the sun.

"In fact, I think it's sort of impossible to explain. . . ."

Freddie Arbuthnot's chin-up smile was nice.

She said, "Buzz off, Fletcher."

There were only two empty seats remaining aboard the plane, one in front (next to Sheldon Levi) which Freddie took, and one in back (next to Leona Hatch) which Fletch got.

Leona Hatch watched him closely while he took off his coat, sat down, and buckled his seat belt.

"I'll swear I've met you before," Leona Hatch said. "Somewhere. . . ."

Five rows in front of him, Freddie's golden head was already buried in a copy of *Newsworld* magazine.

Leona Hatch continued to stare at him.

"What's your name?"

"Fletch."

"What's your full name?"

"Fletcher."

"What's your first name?"

"Irwin."

"What?"

"Irwin. Irwin Fletcher. People call me Fletch."

You're cool Fletch. You're witty, sophisticated, and completely irresistible. Your new assignment is to track down a multimillion-dollar art heist.

But there's this lovely dead blonde in your apartment, and all the evidence points to only one person ...

And you don't think you did it. The police think otherwise, so you'd better find the murderer yourself, or else ...

Confess,
Fletch

GREGORY MCDONALD
Author of FLETCH

 75630/$2.25   FESS 4-80

ROBERT CORMIER
AFTER THE FIRST DEATH

A wave of terror sweeps through a New England town
when a group of masked men hijack a school bus and
demand a huge ransom, the release of political
prisoners, and something more...

Inner Delta: code name for a top secret
counter-espionage agency. Unless it is dismantled,
the children will die, one at a time.

Now, high on a bridge outside of town, a deadly
drama unfolds in which a beautiful blonde bus
driver, a 16-year old terrorist, and the son of the
head of Inner Delta will all learn that it is possible
to die more than once.

AVON 48562 $2.25

AF 4-80